Fated by Fire

Fires of Passion Burn from Within

Dragon Fire Series, Book 1

Kelly Cozzone

Copyright

This book is a work of fiction. The characters, incidents, and dialogue are drawn from the author's imagination and are not to be construed as real. Any resemblance to actual events or persons, living or dead, is entirely coincidental.

Fated by Fire. Copyright 2016 ©

All rights reserved under International and Pan-American American Copyright Conventions. By Payment of the required fees, you have been granted the non-exclusive right to access and read the text of this eBook on screen. No part of this text may be reproduced, transmitted, down-loaded, decompiled, reverse engineered, or stored in or introduced into any information storage and retrieval system, in any form or by any means, whether electronic or mechanical, now known or hereinafter invented, without the express written permission of the author.

First Edition
Book #1 of Dragon Fire Series
All Rights Reserved
ISBN-13: 978-1537181905
ISBN-10: 1537181904
Published in the United States
Cover Design by: JC Clarke of The Graphics Shed
Editing by: Laura Shaw and Kim Huther of Wordsmith Proofreading Services
http://kellycozzone.weebly.com/

KELLY
COZZONE

Welsh words and their English Translations

Tad	Father
Mam	Mother
Un annwyl	Cherished One
Ddraig Wen	White dragon
Fy nghalon	My heart
Fi cariad I chi	I love you
Pwll	Mine
Fy bopeth	My everything
Ei popeth	His everything

Whilst looking down upon his realm, the noble crimson dragon contemplated the might of his dominion. His omniscient gaze cast a shadow over the expansive rolling hillocks of Dinas Emrys. His sole purpose for living was the protection of his king.

His clan's support and devotion to the exalted King Arthur led him to insist on rewarding them. To this end, the mystical Merlin blessed them with the gift of dragon-shifting and immortality. Merlin's bequest ensured his clan's continuity and strength. Thus the humble Owain Cadell rose up into the mighty red dragon destined to rule over all the dragons of the world.

The powerful Draig ascended the mountain to its peak. His two glorious and majestic wings were outstretched behind him revealing, the luminous gold plates that covered them. Spread wide, they blocked out the rays streaming from the sun. The same golden scales guarded the dignified dragon's chest, like a suit of shimmering armor prepared for war. They guaranteed protection for his heart that burned like the fires of his righteous lineage.

The golden scales were flanked by thousands of scarlet plates. The symbol of his clan's near royal heritage, and a trait that passed down through the generations from heir to heir. The most striking feature of this statuesque flying deity were its honey amber eyes. They brought an air of warmth to the imposing being. While seeming soft in nature, they shone with the bold and vivid inferno of his spirit. This titan, the heir of the blazing red dragons, would fight to the death to guard his people and his king.

Chapter One

Jolted awake, Gareth Cadell sat straight up in bed, his naked body tangled in the sheets. His cock, thick and hard, throbbed painfully, needing release. Covered in sweat, his bare chest glistened in the early morning light. Its droplets trailing a delicious path down his abdomen. His heart raced, pounding in his ears. Senses on high alert, he reached out with his mind, scanning the room for anything that shouldn't be there. Nothing, but silence taunted him.

"*Her,*" his dragon roared. Snarling, his beast caused the blood running through his body to boil in its rage. "*Pwll,*" it repeated over and over in his head. *Mine,* echoed in his mind, as the vision of the woman from his dream trembling in fear, flashed before him.

The woman, with her long flowing black hair and piercing blue eyes, haunted him day and night. Her essence swirled around him so that he could almost feel her, smell her, and taste her. *His woman.*

Since his teens, he'd known that somewhere in the world, his soul mate awaited him. Every dragon had its perfect mate, the feminine to his masculine. When merged, the mating bond would guarantee their lines and their eternity. It was the way of the gods and their assurance to people that the powerful clans would continue.

His dragon had longed for her, for years, and it had searched endlessly. Her very essence had called to him even before she was born. He burned for her, ached for her, and knew the moment she had entered the world. Everything he'd waited for, the peace, the serenity, and the passion, was within his grasp. The dragon heir needed the calm their mating would bring.

The first images he had of her were nothing more than a flicker of the blackness of her hair. The dreams evolved into full-blown visions of her. Gareth struggled with the conflicting pictures of her that pierced his dreams. Sometimes she was happy and laughing, and then terrifying ones of her bleeding and hurt would eclipse everything.

Seeing her near death in his nightmares tore out his heart and infuriated his dragon. The realization that his eternity could be over before he found his mate, enraged them both. Their survival, their destiny, depended on her survival.

After the latest horrors in his sleep, he understood without a doubt, that he was running out of time. With her life dangling perilously close to death, he couldn't let anything get in the way of saving his mate. He had to move soon and ensure her protection. The one thing he knew with absolute certainty was that no one would touch his woman, not as long as he drew breath!

Shoving himself upright, he threw his legs over the side of the bed and rubbed his eyes. He shook his head to clear his dark thoughts, understanding that dwelling on the position he found himself in wasn't going to help anyone, especially his mate.

Stretching his arms over his head, frustration with the direction his life was going boiled his blood. His mate required his undivided attention, but he wasn't in a place to give it to her. Hell, he didn't even know who she was. Anger coursed through him as he stomped into the bathroom, turning the shower to scalding hot. As he stepped under the water, it burned as it cascaded down his body, turning his skin red.

While he adjusted to the scorching heat of the water, it caressed every inch as it flowed down the natural lines of his torso. The heat eased the tension in his muscles, and he felt himself slowly relax. Dropping his head, he let the water beat down on the back of his neck.

When the water started to cool, he quickly washed and rinsed the soap from his body. Shutting off the water, he stepped out, grabbing a towel. As he dried himself, he caught his reflection in the mirror.

The birthmark on his arm had transformed itself as he aged. By the time he'd reached his eighteenth birthday, the fierce red dragon, with its golden wings spread majestically, had encircled his upper arm. Its talons were poised, ready to slash its prey, and its amber eyes, which were the exact shade of his own, burned. The glorious dragon was the spitting image of his inner beast. The mark acted as a constant reminder that he needed to keep his responsibilities and family legacy at the forefront of his thoughts.

He slipped into his clothes as his mind wandered to his mate. He knew she wasn't in close proximity to him because he couldn't sense her; and yet, even with the distance, he felt the pull of his dragon towards her. Closing his eyes, he could conjure her image perfectly as if he'd been shown a photo.

Her long black hair flowed down her back, curling at the bottom. He imagined it would feel as soft and silky in his hand as it looked in his mind. Her icy blue eyes pierced his dreams and demanded his attention. He had no doubt that he would know her the moment his gaze landed on her. His dragon would recognize the one that destiny had created for him.

His dragon snorted and the mark around his arm heated at the thought of claiming his mate. "Calm yourself," he ordered his beast. The restlessness of his dragon tested his patience to the core. The two had waged an internal battle for months. One they would continue to wage until they were finally able to claim their mate.

I have to find her before the ddraig wen is able to get their hands on her. If Maelon Godwin, the heir of the White Dragon clan, got to her first, his eternity would be lost. As long as they both lived, his future lay before him, but if she died, he would lose his immortality. *It's the only way to kill a dragon without cutting off its head.*

If he died, the *ddraig wen* would finally claim his lands and his people. Death and destruction would follow in its wake. *I will not allow that to be my legacy.*

Chapter Two

Fighting the urge to pace around her kitchen, Carys Cadell felt the turmoil of her people. The security of their clan was being threatened, for the first time in over a millennium. Their fate rested on the shoulders of a raven-haired beauty.

The strength of her being would determine if they survived. The woman's destiny, set in motion long before any of them had been born, would be their salvation or their destruction.

Breathing deeply, she peered out the window and her gaze took in the beauty of her home, Dinas Emrys. Located in northwest Wales, the rocky and wooded hill contrasted in hard and soft. It portrayed their people, their hard exterior paired with the beauty of their heart.

Its rocky cliffs gave way to the green rolling woods filled with the special trees and flowers of the Welsh people. Their scent, mingled with the damp earthen aroma, filled the air, swirling through the open window. She breathed deeply, allowing the magic of the land to wrap around her and soothe her soul. The window allowed her to stare out at the vivid blue sky trying to break through the constant ring of fog.

The Cadell ancestors had lived in, and protected Dinas Emrys, since the time of King Arthur. Due to their fierce support of him, Merlin, the Master Wizard, had blessed the Red Dragon clan by creating the first dragon shifter, Owain Cadell. His precious gift ensured their survival. The land around Dinas Emrys was holy, the sacred place of all the red dragons.

Sensing the presence of her son, she smiled. Her dragon warmed with the love for their first born. "Gareth, when do you leave for Boston?"

"*Mam*, please come and sit with me," he asked noticing the tension in her stance that she tried to hide. "We've talked about this trip for weeks. You know that I'm leaving later today. Now, tell me, what has you so upset?" Gareth questioned softly. Peering at his mother, their bond made it possible for him to feel the anxiety and stress that radiated from her slender body. Her eyes that were normally a sparkling green were haunted by shadows. Wrinkles deepened with her frown and the circles of no sleep surrounded her eyes. "Have you had one of your visions?"

Giving in to his request, Carys sat down tensely on the edge of a chair. Wringing a tea towel in her hands, she blatantly ignored his question. The last thing she wanted to discuss with him was her visions. They were her burden to bear. The sacrifice she willingly accepted for her family. "I'm worried that now isn't a good time for you to leave the country."

Meeting his gaze, she continued, "I'm scared about what will happen while you are so far away from the family. You know that there is a good possibility that Maelon will follow you to Boston." Their family was stronger when they were together. It was their bond that funneled their strength and gave them the edge they needed to maintain their realm.

Kneeling down in front of his mother, he took the towel from her. Laying it aside, he wrapped her hands in his. Running his finger along her delicate hand, he felt the love for his mother that grew stronger with each passing year. She was the calming force in their clan. She was the one that all the clansmen and women went to for sage advice. Seeing her in this state of fear stole his breath. It was difficult for him to watch his strong, wise mother struggle with the future's unknown. He knew if her visions were awful enough to upset her this much, it didn't bode well for their realm.

"Where is this coming from? There hasn't been any trouble with the Godwin's in over fifteen-hundred years. None of the other dragon clan has shown an ounce of any uprising to come," he asked, knowing from his own visions that he was lying to her. "The number of white dragons has diminished to the point where they couldn't harm us even if they wanted to. The feud is dead and buried."

"That's where you're wrong, *un annwyl*. I feel them stirring in my blood, and in here," she said, pointing to her heart. "I know you think I'm spewing the ramblings of an old woman, but I know of what I speak. You don't understand all that our family went through to fight off the *ddraig wen*." Her inner beast roared at the mention of the white dragons. The beast's mark around her upper arm burned as her dragon demanded to be called forth. Quieting her mind, she forced feelings of peace and calm at her dragon. The green eyes in her mark glowed, lighting beneath her shirt sleeve.

Seeing the glow, Gareth knew his mother's dragon was on edge. She hadn't been letting her beast out and it was weakening her. "Mother, when is the last time you let your dragon free?"

"That's not important. What *is* important is protecting this clan. Nothing else matters."

"It is important," he whispered. "She needs to be allowed to be free. You're blocking her and her strength. You can't continue to ignore what is natural. We need her, and you, at your strongest."

Shaking her head, she murmured, "Don't you feel their pull? Don't you feel them coming together?"

"Yes, you know I do. I'm not immune to what the *ddraig wen* can do. You think I don't understand, but I know all about the war we waged against the white dragons. They invaded, trying to take our land and our people. They tried to overthrow our rule, but they didn't succeed. A Cadell has reigned and protected Dinas Emrys ever since," he recited, even as the vision of Maelon attacking his mate flashed in his mind, ensuring he knew what a dangerous path he was on.

"Father explained it all in great detail to me. I'm not blind to our history or our family's legacy. Why would they consider attacking us after all this time? Everything is going to be fine. Besides, I'm not going to be gone long. I only have to inspect the new office. I'll be home before you know it, and if Maelon ends up in Boston, I'll deal with him." Rising to his feet, he kissed the top of her head before turning to walk away. Hearing her whisper his name, he paused.

"Does your blood not warm at the thought of them? Remember, love, your destiny was fated by fire. *Ddraig wen* will rise again. Prophesy foretells it and my dragon feels it, just as I'm sure yours does. Do not ignore your heart when your brain doubts. *She* holds the key! *She* will either be our protector or our downfall."

"Mam, *she* will be everything for us."

Watching her son walk out the door, she prayed he was right, but fear churned in her stomach. If Maelon got to her son's mate first, their fate was sealed. It was the only way for the Godwin's to defeat them. They had to

kill the woman, the one destiny
created for her son. The one created to
save their people.

Chapter Three

Stepping out of the plane, Gareth Cadell paused to drop his sunglasses down onto his nose. Even in late October, the sun was still bright. It poured its healing light down on the Earth. Though the temperatures in Boston were already getting colder, the freezing temperatures still hadn't hit. The sunlight streamed through the clouds, creating a kaleidoscope of color on the crisp fall day. Thankfully, the dragon blood running through his veins kept his body warm, and he didn't feel the chill in the air.

Snow would soon cover the ground, and the trees would drip with icicles while snow flurries filled the sky. Thankfully, he was missing the air that would be so cold that he would be able to see his breath every time he exhaled. Peering around the airport, he caught sight of men scurrying around trying to do their jobs in the chilly wind.

Making his way down the steps, he grinned at his American attorney, Allen Parker. The man was standing by the car and it was obvious that he was cold. Chuckling to himself, he knew that as someone new to the Boston area, Allen felt the chill more than a normal Bostonian. As he waited for Gareth to approach, he blew his heated breath into his hands.

He almost felt bad for asking his attorney to meet his plane, but Allen handled all of the details involved in opening the American branch of his family's business, Cadell Industries, and he didn't want to waste a minute of the trip. The future of their company rested on the expansion project he was working on.

Cadell Industries had grown into a successful shipping company that had been started by his grandfather, Emery Cadell. Emery was the son of the great Owain Cadell, the man who led the battle against the invading white dragons, earning honor and blessings on their entire clan. Owain Cadell had been the one blessed by Merlin and had become their first dragon shifter. When Owain had died, dragons came from around the world to honor him. It was a somber affair that went on for weeks.

Gareth slung his bag over his shoulder as he headed toward his attorney and the car. Stopping at its side, he extended his hand, "Hi, Allen. Thanks for meeting me. I see you're still adjusting to the cold of the Northeast."

Returning the handshake, Allen sized up his employer. Dressed in Armani, Gareth oozed money and power. "My body still remembers the warmth of Florida. I'm dreading the coming winter. I was happy to meet you." Leading the way to the car, he rattled off all of the information Gareth had requested.

"Your meeting with Cadence de Luca is set for nine in the morning. After you've introduced yourself to her and gone over the books, she'll show you around the office." Stowing Gareth's bags in the trunk, he continued to relay the information. "The warehouse expects you either tomorrow afternoon or first thing the next morning. You'll be able to inspect the warehouse and the dock, as well as go over their processes. I've instituted all of the standard operating procedures you sent me. Once you approve everything and sign off on all we've done, they'll be ready to open for business Monday morning."

Sliding into the car, Gareth was thrilled to learn everything was on schedule and moving forward smoothly. "Excellent! You've been a lifesaver during this expansion. We wouldn't even be close to ready for the opening without you. Now, tell me about Ms. De Luca. What should I expect?" he asked. He'd been hesitant to hire someone to run this arm of the company without having actually met them. Yet, after seeing her credentials and speaking to her references, he went ahead with the decision to offer her the job. Her references had been impeccable, but more importantly, she'd impressed his father, and that was almost impossible to do.

"She's going to be a huge asset to Cadell Industries. She's smart, and knows the shipping industry inside and out. We were lucky to steal her away from our competitors, however…" he paused, trying to figure out how to best explain her less than favorable side.

"However, what?" he asked.

"However, she's also stubborn and pigheaded when she thinks she's right. Not to mention, I think she may have minored in sarcasm in college."

Laughing at his description, Gareth couldn't wait to meet the woman who could render his attorney speechless which wasn't an easy feat. He hoped he'd be able to witness it in person. *Anyone who can accomplish that is someone I must have on my side.*

Instantly, his dragon roared in his head at the thoughts he had towards a woman who wasn't his mate. *Give it a rest,* he ordered his beast. *I'm not betraying our mate!* Chuffing in frustration, his dragon let him know how unhappy it was.

"You laugh, but I'm telling you, she's fierce," Allen said, chuckling.

Sipping her coffee, Cadence de Luca scanned the paperwork from her grandmother's safety deposit box spread out on her coffee table. Chewing on her bottom lip, she analyzed the information for the hundredth time. Tucking her feet under her, she leaned back against the cushions and closed her eyes.

Everything she'd read in her grandmother's papers exhausted her. She didn't know what to make of all the crazy things she'd learned. Opening her eyes, she spied the coffee cup she'd set on the table. She needed the boost she'd get from the caffeine, and forced herself not to grab it up and gulp it down.

Nothing in her grandmother's papers made sense. Dealing with the loss of the only person she had growing up was hard enough, but trying to understand the life her Nana lived was almost impossible. In addition to the safety deposit box, she'd found an old cardboard box shoved into the back of her grandmother's attic. It was full of magical items, a wand, candles, talismans, and a spell book. All strange items, for her grandmother to own, but what shocked her most was the letter her grandmother had left for her.

The letter from her grandmother had been hidden in

the bottom of the safety deposit box and it was addressed to her. No matter how hard she worked to understand, the letter continued to confuse her. The letter revealed that the members of her family were witches. How was it possible for her grandmother to think they were witches and she didn't know? Witches didn't exist. Magic was nothing but fantasy.

    Was her grandmother delusional? She had seemed so coherent, even at the end. If it hadn't been for cancer, her Nana would still be with her. So where did this crazy idea come from? One large scroll confused her even further. It was a handwritten family tree that went all the way back to the late fifth century. It seemed surreal to her to even imagine that anyone could trace their family tree back that far.

Even crazier than the length of the family tree was the name at the top: Merlin, the famed sorcerer from King Arthur. Surely this had to be some sort of joke. Merlin wasn't even real, how could he possibly be the head of their family. With no family left to ask, Cadence's heart broke at the understanding that she'd never get to the bottom of the strange things she'd discovered.

Needing to get away for a while and clear her thoughts, she decided to head to her favorite pub and have a drink. Slipping into her shoes, she grabbed her bag to stroll through the streets of

Boston. She loved this time of year. The leaves had turned their golden colors and the trees were decorated for the season. Before long, the leaves would be gone and snow and slush would cover the ground.

Halloween was normally her favorite holiday, but with the loss of her grandmother, she just couldn't get into it this year. She hadn't even put up her decorations. The thought of the children at the door trick or treating, and not being able to see her grandmother delight in their costumes saddened her.

Walking into the pub, she hurried to the end of the bar and slid onto a stool. She ordered her normal drink and savored the warmth as the bourbon hit her system.

Chapter Four

After settling into his hotel and having dinner with Allen, Gareth hated the uneasiness piercing his very core. His dragon grew more restless with each passing minute. Thinking a walk and a drink would calm him and his beast, he exited the hotel. As he started off down the street, instead of easing the tension in his muscles, the area at the base of the back of his neck began to burn.

Turning the corner, he discovered a quaint pub and the closer he got, recognition slammed into him, stealing his breath. *Her!* He felt the one woman who destiny had created for him reach out and wrap herself around his soul. She was close, closer than she'd ever been!

Feeling her, his dragon urged him on, straining to be called forth.

Calm yourself, he instructed his beast. It snorted its refusal in return, demanding he locate his mate. Roaring inside, it took everything he had to prevent him from shifting. Pausing, he closed his eyes and focused on his dragon. Forcing calmness at it, he gained control.

As he stood in front of the little pub, he felt her being surge through him, boiling his blood. Emotions he knew would come when he found her pulsed in his chest, stronger than anything he'd ever thought possible. Pushing open the door, he made a beeline for the bar and ordered, "Give me anything you've got on tap." Scanning the area, his eyes fell on the most beautiful blue eyes he'd ever seen, in the mirror behind the bar. His dragon instantly reared its head, straining against his composure.

Heat radiated through his blood and his amber eyes glowed with desire. His cock hardened, straining against his zipper. Lust filled him and the urge to take her was almost unbearable. The attraction was instant, and he knew he'd finally found his other half; his destiny.

Slowly roaming his eyes over the beauty in the mirror, her long black mane blocked part of her face. He itched to reach out and tuck the strands behind her ear so he could see all of her. Unable to tear his gaze away, her eyes flashed a combination of heat and annoyance. A lazy grin crossed his face as he licked his lips.

The bartender slid the beer in front of him and picked up the cash he'd laid on the napkin. Lifting the glass, he sipped as he continued to watch her. Her face flamed under his stare, and he knew she was aware of his presence.

Picking up his glass, he stood up from the stool. Taking his time, he strolled towards her, eyeing the empty stool beside her. Sliding onto it, he turned to face her.

Signaling to the bartender to bring them another round, he stuck out his hand towards her. "I'll grab the next round," he announced, confident she wouldn't be able to refuse to have a drink with him. Her scent filled the air around him, seeping into his soul. She smelled like a meadow after a cleansing rain, reminding him of his home in Wales.

"Not interested," she replied, turning on her stool so that her back was to him. Cadence de Luca fought the pounding of her heart, having realized that she was staring at the most gorgeous man she'd ever seen. His red hair was pulled back in a short, slicked-back tail, and she just knew if she released it from its holder it would curl around her finger. His amber eyes glowed almost gold, and heat hit her core as desire flowed through her body. She felt drawn to him as she had no one else before. *What the hell is wrong with me?*

Grinning, his gaze met hers in the mirror. He'd scented her desire and knew she was as aware of him as he was her. *Mine,* his dragon roared in his head. *I know,* he replied. *Give me a minute,* he argued, fighting to control his beast, who threatened to take her right there in front of God and everyone. Pure, barely controllable desire filled his blood, and her scent shot straight to his cock.

Music blared around him, while couples chatted and enjoyed the atmosphere of the pub, but he couldn't drag his eyes away from her. Fighting his dragon, it took every ounce of willpower he had not to grab her up, throw her over his shoulder, and storm out the front door. His gaze fell on hers in the mirror and his eyes bored into hers. He couldn't walk away. He'd finally found his mate, his

destiny, the one created only for him;
his heart, his soul, his everything.

Chapter Five

Unable to tear her gaze away from him in the mirror, Cadence struggled against the urge to face him. She felt a pull she'd never experienced and felt drawn to him like no man she'd ever met. *Stop it,* she ordered herself. *He's just a man, for crying out loud.*

Yet, the more she watched him the stronger his pull grew. Power emanated from him, showing the warrior she instinctively knew him to be. Enthralled by him, she closed her eyes, dropping the mental guard she normally held tightly shut. She wanted to savor him, wanted to taste him, wanted to feel him.

His energy surrounded her, with love and peace centering her turbulent emotions. *Fy nghalon,* her eyes flew open. "What did you just say?" she growled as her eyes narrowed, piercing and holding his eyes to hers.

"I didn't say anything," he replied, shocked to the depth of his soul. *Surely she didn't hear the grumblings of my dragon.* No mate could hear the dragon until the bonding ceremony. *That's impossible.*

"I heard you," she accused. "What was that language?" Staring at him, she felt his unease, aware that he knew exactly what she was talking about. But his confusion seemed real, and it reached out to her, sliding over her body as a caress. Her neck burned as if a flame had marked her. Her breath caught as fear, lust, and pain washed over her. Needing to get away from him, she slid off the stool, taking her purse.

Turning, her eyes met his, and his turmoil mirrored her own. With the heat on the back of her neck burning hotter, she fled out the front door and into the night.

Shadows reached across the sidewalk as she hurried down the darkened concrete. Dim streetlights lit the way, and pale moonlight sent shadows dancing across the road. Trees rustled in the night breeze, giving the air an eerie chill. "Only four blocks, stay calm." She focused on her surroundings as she raced towards her apartment, trying to ignore the conflicting emotions battling inside her. A block from her home she came to a standstill, panic surging through her.

The feeling of being watched pierced her body. Narrowing her eyes, she peered into the darkness, searching for the source of her fear. Unable to see anything, she relied on her senses. Forcing her eyes shut, she opened her mind. In seconds, malevolence sent goosebumps down her arms. Turning towards the blackness, the evil projected back at her drilled dread and fear into her.

As Gareth threw open the door to the pub, he felt the shift in the air. *Maelon, you son of a bitch.* "No, no, no," he roared, *run, love, don't stop!* He sent out telepathically, hoping she'd hear him again. His dragon drove him faster, urging him on. Sprinting in her direction, he reached out to Maelon in his mind. *Back off,* basdun*! Hurt her, and I will kill you!*

He heard the taunting laughter, and rage surged through him. Pushing himself harder, he gathered his dragon magic and channeled it towards his mate. *Please work*, he prayed. *Give her the strength to get away.*

He knew instantly the only way to stop Maelon was to kill him. He had no doubt that as long as the *ddraig wen* heir lived, his mate would never be safe. The connection to Maelon triggered his dragon's fighting mode. He could feel it trying to overpower his control and spring forward. Defending its mate was all it cared about. Roaring in his head, his dragon vowed to end the threat against *ei popeth*.

As her apartment building came into view, Cadence felt a surge of energy and sprang forward. Forcing her legs to go faster, the pure evil that surrounded her chilled her blood. Reaching her building, she used the renewed power to take the steps two at a time, and flew through the front door, slamming it behind her. Bending over at the waist, her body slumped against the door as she tried to catch her breath.

Slipping her hand under her shirt, she pulled out the necklace her grandmother had given her on her sixteenth birthday. It was her talisman and a link to the grandmother she'd loved more than anything. When her beloved Nana passed, it was how she kept her alive, and she could feel her healing energy flowing through it.

Wrapping her fingers around the beautiful stone, she felt it grow warm, as peace and protection encircled her. The fear and panic gripping her eased, freeing her from its stronghold. As her soul settled and her breathing evened out, she walked the short distance down the hall to her apartment.

Inserting the key into the lock, Cadence struggled to explain away everything that had just happened. From the strong pull of the mystery man at the bar, to the shocking knowledge that something dangerous followed her home, she didn't know which scared her more.

Dropping down onto her couch, her head fell back onto the cushion. The stress of the night triggered her desire to see her family, to feel her grandmother's arms wrap around her. It was moments like this that deepened the grief she had suffered at their deaths. With no one left to comfort her, she felt the sorrow in her soul. So much had been left unsaid, so much she didn't know.

Flying up the front steps, Gareth burst into the foyer of her apartment building. Instinctively knowing which door she was behind, he banged on it. "Please open the door. I need to know that you're alright," he shouted. *Enjoy her now, Gareth...she shall be mine soon.* Maelon's taunt pierced his heart. *"You'll never have her. I'll kill you first,* Gareth promised.

Fear turned her stomach over as she heard a man's voice yelling. "Leave me alone!"

Laying his hand on the door, Gareth leaned forward until his forehead touched the wood, "I just need to make sure that you're okay." His dragon all but ordered him to break down the door and get to her.

His stomach clenched with worry. He could hear the fear and sadness in her voice, and the desire to hold her stormed through him.

"I'm fine… Go away!" she demanded. "Please, I just want to be alone." Tears threatened to fall and grief tickled the back of her throat. Curling up on the couch, she wrapped her hand around her talisman for comfort.

Feeling her sorrow in his gut, it stole his breath. He wanted to comfort her but knew she'd never allow it. It was too soon for her to turn to him and it tore his heart out. He needed to be the one to hold her and wipe away her tears.

Exhaling loudly in frustration, Gareth turned and walked out into the night. Standing in the shadows, he peered at her darkened apartment, waiting for the lights to come on. Noticing a small light illuminate the window, he wished she'd let him in.

Using his dragon senses, he searched the area for any sign of Maelon Godwin. He let out a breath, unaware he'd been holding it, after finding no trace of the man destined to destroy him.

Settling in for the night, he refused to consider leaving her unprotected. Maelon wouldn't go far, and the idea of him getting to his mate caused his stomach to knot in dread.

Chapter Six

The sunlight streaming through the windows pierced Cadence's eyelids, signaling to her body that it was time to get up. After the crazy night she'd had, her sleep had been full of strange dreams. One had been about the man from the bar, and it had been one hot, sexually powerful dream that left her wanting and wet with desire.

The most vivid dream, however, had been about her grandmother. Cadence had been standing in a lush green meadow and could see her Nana on the other side. When her grandmother walked away, she'd followed her into the woods to an amazingly beautiful waterfall. The vibrant blue water cascaded over the rocks, landing in a deep blue pool. She could see her grandmother telling her something, but she couldn't hear her words. The closer she got, the more her grandmother faded away.

She'd awoken sweaty and sexually frustrated, but also deeply sad, with the loss of her grandmother weighing heavily upon her. Shaking her head to dispel her dark thoughts, she threw off the covers and stormed into the bathroom to get ready for work.

Outside, as the sun rose, Gareth couldn't keep his mind off of the stunning beauty who had turned out to be his mate. His visions had shown him how gorgeous she was, but he hadn't expected the purity of her soul. When she'd slept, her mental guards had slipped away, allowing him to get a better sense of her.

She haunted his dreams, and no matter how hard he tried, he couldn't stop his thoughts from turning to her. During the night, he'd discovered something he hadn't expected, white magic. It swirled around her, and yet he suspected she didn't know. She gave no indication that she had the ability to funnel her magic.

Finding his mate on a business trip to Boston had been a surprise, the magic had been a surprise, but having her rebuke his advances almost immediately unsettled him. "How the hell did she fight the need?"

She should have felt every ounce of desire that he did. *Could fate be wrong?* Did his mate not recognize him? "It's not possible," he told himself. "I know how she feels in my soul, and how my heart beats for her. How can she not feel it? How is it that I know where she lives, but I don't know her name?" Frustrated, he paced back and forth outside her apartment.

Tormented by her rejection, his dragon urged him to find her again, to go to her and claim her. It was getting harder to focus on his job when danger and uncertainty surrounded his mate. *How do I claim someone who can walk away from me? How do I make her mine? How do I keep her safe?*

Hearing the door open, he stepped behind a tree and watched as she exited her building. His breath caught as she stood on the sidewalk, his gaze traveling her body from the top of her head, with her shiny black hair down her back. His eyes ran over her tight ass, past her perfectly shaped legs, to the hottest pair of stilettos he'd ever seen.

His erection throbbed in his pants, forcing him to adjust himself. Seeing the approaching cab, he was torn between the need to follow her and to attend his business meeting. His family obligation pulled at him, and yet his dragon fought to follow his mate.

As the cab drove off, he made the decision to go to his meeting, and end it as quickly as possible so he could get back to his mate. He couldn't bear the thought of leaving her unprotected and vulnerable. It sent waves of fear coursing through his body.

Racing back to his hotel, he took a quick shower. Peering into the mirror hanging on the wall, his haunted eyes stared back. He could still smell her, and it drove desire through him. Walking away from her home that morning had taken every ounce of willpower he had.

Between her pull and his dragon's desire, he'd barely refused his dragon the release he'd demanded. Allowing his beast its freedom in the middle of Boston was a risk he couldn't take. He had to keep it together and deny his dragon its natural urges. Straightening his tie, he grabbed his briefcase and headed out for his meeting.

Walking into the main lobby of Cadell Industries Gareth took everything in, thrilled by the feel of it. Decorated in the golden tans and reds of his clan, the furniture was simple but elegant. The family crest hung on the wall behind the front desk. *Mother will love it.* Turning to inspect the rest of the room, it reminded him of the main office in Wales. *They've managed to capture the essence of our people without even knowing it,* he thought in wonder.

Seeing the woman at the reception desk, he briskly walked up to her. "I'm here to see Ms. de Luca." *Time to get this meeting over with I need to get back to my mate.* His dragon roared his approval.

"Do you have an appointment?" Her eyelashes fluttered as she slowly looked him up and down, and her desire filled the air around him. Making no effort to disguise her attraction, she licked her lower lip, tilted her head to the side, and continued her appraisal of him.

Gareth watched as she undressed him with her eyes, and her unspoken offer annoyed him. In the past, he might have considered taking her up but not now. Not since he'd finally found the one destiny had created just for him. Now all he wanted to do was get the meeting out of the way as quickly as possible, and her innuendos were taking up time he didn't have.

"Tell her it's Gareth Cadell," he responded, meeting her direct gaze. His harsh expression let her know he wasn't interested in what she was offering without saying a word.

Wide-eyed and embarrassed at his rejection, she quickly dialed the phone, whispering into the handset. Seconds later, she hung up and jumped from her chair, "Right this way, Mr. Cadell. Ms. de Luca is waiting for you." Scurrying down the hallway, she led him to the conference room.

Following behind her as she raced up the hall, his thoughts turned to his mate. He prayed she was somewhere Maelon couldn't get to her, and safe, at least for the moment. He felt her magnetic energy pulling at him and wondered at the strength of it. He knew he would have the ability to sense her but it was as if she was in close proximity to him.

She had to be nearby in order for him to feel her confusion, slithering up his spine. Her fear penetrated his heart like a knife. The fact that he'd been the one to cause her the terror and turmoil infuriated him. He knew she was in danger because of him. Rage boiled up, tempting his dragon.

By the time the receptionist stopped at the closed conference room door, he was engaged in a battle of wills with his dragon. His beast wasn't interested in the meeting, all it cared about was getting to their mate before Maelon did.

The receptionist quickly opened the door and stepped aside to allow him to enter.

The minute the door swung open, Gareth's eyes landed on the shocked gaze of his soul mate. Unable to believe she was standing right in front of him, his body reacted the same way it had the night before. His neck burned and his dragon roared in its pleasure. His dick catapulted up, standing proudly at attention. It demanded that she notice it.

"You!" she gasped when the man of her erotic dreams stepped into the room.

Chapter Seven

Cadence de Luca's head snapped around at the sound of the opening door. She found herself staring into the exquisite amber eyes of the man she'd been astonishingly enticed by the night before. *Holy shit...not good Cadence, so not good. Confronted with the fact that the man who had starred in a long, restless night of hotter than hell sex dreams stood in her office, she began to panic.*

Her heart pounded in her ears, and her palms grew slick with sweat. The sudden urge to pace strained her control. Unconsciously chewing on her bottom lip, she attempted to figure out how to handle the situation the right way. *Why me? Why did he have to be Gareth Cadell? Great job, Cadence, let's just lust after our new boss, why don't we? That's always a fantastic career move,* she silently chastised herself. Taking a deep breath to settle her nerves, she took a step forward and extended her hand. "Mr. Cadell, welcome to Cadell Industries. I'm Cadence de Luca."

"Ms. de Luca, fancy meeting you here." Striding across the room, he struggled to keep his mindset on the job and not on the fact that his mate was standing in front of him. He couldn't believe that the last several months his mate had been right here under his nose. He could kick himself for not having found her sooner.

Torn between excitement and frustration, he set his briefcase down on the desk and wiped his face clear of emotion. Accepting her handshake, the energy between them sent a spark flying up his arm. Feeling her move to withdraw, he gripped her hand tighter, enjoying the lust-filled look that crossed her face. "Are you okay?" His business meeting became unimportant, as the one thing he now had to focus on, was keeping Cadence safe. Still unable to understand how she had managed to deny him the night before, her wellbeing became his number one priority.

Staring dumbfounded at her new boss, Cadence's stomach tightened and anxiety threatened to bulldoze over her. She tried to extract her hand from his but he tightened his grip, making it impossible. Strong chemistry caused electricity to flow between them, shooting straight to the center of her core.

After the intense and now utterly embarrassing run-in with him the night before, her body refused to listen to her. Its uncharacteristic response to him had her praying for composure. "Mr. Cadell, about last night, I'm…," she stammered.

"It's Gareth," he interrupted gruffly. "Are you okay?" Glancing at her, his gaze landed on her full luscious lips, lips that begged to be kissed and devoured. Eyes drawn to her mouth, his mind conjured a vision of them surrounding his cock. Her tongue darted out to lick her bottom lip, causing his dick to swell and harden to its thick and full, painful length.

Ignoring the passion igniting his blood, he pushed himself to focus on her, patiently waiting for her to respond. Unable to decide which emotion was going to win, anger at the situation they were in or lust, he silently vowed to wait her out. Otherwise, he was going to throw her down on the table and take her right there in the conference room. Showing calm that he didn't feel he sat down at the table.

His dragon demanded that he forget the question and focus on claiming their mate. *Would you please stop! I know what you want, but it isn't the right time.* He could feel the heat from his dragon's disapproval burning on his arm as the beast squeezed him.

Attempting not to give in to the emotions determined to make her crazy, she gingerly sat down across from him at the conference table. She could feel his eyes on her, scrutinizing her. Unable to stand the doubt his appraisal was causing, she dropped her head down onto her hands.

He knew he couldn't help her. He could feel the waves of confusion emanating from her. It hurt his heart to know he was the reason she was struggling, but not being able to see her face gave him the perfect ability to watch her, to savor her scent.

Being this close to her not only calmed him, but it calmed his beast as well. It grounded the two of them in a way they'd never experienced. He wasn't going to let anyone or anything take her away from him.

Conflicting emotions filled Cadence as she felt his eyes boring into her. On one hand, she felt safe, protected even, and on the other, she could barely stand the sexual pull. The attraction settled deep in her soul and she tried not to picture him naked. "Okay, why are you staring at me?"

"I'm waiting for you to answer my question," he challenged, enjoying her discomfort when he scented her desire. His mind conjured a vision of the two of them sealing their bond. Ignited in passion, he licked his lips in anticipation. Catching her looking at him, he replied, "I'm ready to listen to you."

"Then what did I just say?" she asked, knowing he hadn't heard one word she'd said. His piercing amber eyes reflected the same passion building in her. She fidgeted in her seat, ignoring the heat burning between her legs.

His cheeks heated when he realized he'd been caught not paying attention. *How the hell am I supposed to focus on anything when she's right there?* His dragon agreed, encouraging him to forget everything and solve their problem. They had to claim their mate before Maelon found her.

"Cadence," he whispered, needing her attention to be focused on him. "Look at me," he ordered. "I tried to ignore this, but we have to deal with it. We won't get anything accomplished until we do." Peering at her, he waited for her response. It felt as if he and his dragon were holding their collective breaths.

Knowing exactly what he was talking about, she refused to look up. The intense attraction between them was obvious, and his energy seemed to wrap around her like a cocoon. It made her feel as if nothing could ever hurt her again which, in itself, was strange. She'd never had anyone touch her the same way except her grandmother. "I don't know what 'it' is, but I doubt it's more important than getting your company up and running," she deflected.

"Cadence, look at me. Nothing is more important than what is going on between us, *un annwyl*." Reaching across the table, he lifted her chin with his finger until her eyes met his. "And I mean nothing."

Gasping, his words paralyzed her. Her heart felt as if it would burst, and in an instant, a distant memory of her grandmother slammed into her. She'd been only a child when she'd entered her grandmother's bedroom without knocking.

Her grandmother had been kneeling in front of a small altar adorned with flower petals and candles. She'd been chanting in a language Cadence hadn't recognized at the time, but now knew to be

Welsh. When her grandmother realized she was there, she'd uttered the same words. "What does that mean? I've heard it before."

Taking her hand in his, his thumb moved in small circles across the skin. "*Un annwyl* means 'cherished one', and you are cherished by me, Cadence."

"That's not possible…, you don't even know me," she quipped, dismissing his claim. "We only met last night. There's no way I matter that much to you already." Shaking her head, she wanted to yank her hand out of his grasp but something stopped her. Something deep inside her knew he spoke the truth. She didn't know how she knew it, but something her grandmother used to say made her believe him even though she didn't want to. *You're destined for a long life full of love, and spent with a man you won't see coming. One day, our family legacy will reveal itself to you. You must be prepared to face the life our ancestors ensured.*

At the time, Cadence had thought it was just the hopes and dreams of an old woman, but now she had no doubt her life had just changed forever.

Standing, Gareth pulled her to her feet. "Let's get out of here. We have a lot to talk about and we're running out of time."

"What does that mean? Why are we running out of time?" She felt an incapacitating fear in the pit of her stomach. Something about his body language and the look in his eyes filled her with terror.

"Everything will be okay, but we have to leave now." He'd felt Maelon trying to connect with him for the last hour. He was getting desperate, and Gareth wasn't sure how long it would be before he made his presence known. He had to deal with Cadence and convince her of the mating between them before that happened. "I promise, *Fy nghalon*, I'll explain everything to you soon."

Chapter Eight

Throwing open the front door of Cadell Industries, Gareth rested his hand on the small of her back and escorted her out. Her skin burned at his touch, the heat scorching them both. Having her at his side felt more right than anything he'd ever imagined. Her head came up to his shoulders, and she fit up against him perfectly.

He steered her quickly toward his waiting car and helped her inside. Scanning the area for anything out of place, he slid inside and gave the driver her address. Tossing up a silent prayer, he hoped with all that was holy that he had enough time before Maelon made his move. Hearing her inhale, he jerked around to face her as the car shot away from the street.

"What the hell is going on? Gareth, you're scaring me!" Her hands trembled as she toyed with the hem of her skirt. The entire situation had her insides all twisted up. Everything was so disorienting. None of it made any sense. Yesterday, the only thing she had to worry about was meeting her new boss. Now, her boss turned out to be a sexually exciting and primal man she couldn't help lusting after and he was somehow crazy about her. Complicating matters more, they were in some kind of danger.

Reaching up to close her hand around her necklace, she was driven to soak up the serenity of her talisman. The moment her fingers encircled the stone, she could sense something dark and treacherous surrounding them. Squeezing tighter, she waited for the calm that would eventually come.

"Where did you get that?" Gareth questioned as something niggled at the back of his mind. He'd seen that type of talisman before, but couldn't put his finger on where.

"It was my grandmother's. She gave it to me for my sixteenth birthday, and I have never taken it off," she replied, lifting the necklace for him to get a closer look. "It's the last thing I have connecting me to her and I'm not ready to let go of her yet."

The minute her fingers opened and he could see the entire pendant, understanding shot through him. He finally understood how she was able to hear his dragon before the mating ceremony and why she had heard the language of his ancestors before he uttered it.

"Cadence, what do you know about the symbol in the center of the stone?"

"The symbol… I don't know anything about it. All my grandmother would ever say was that one day it would all make sense. It seems like she left me in the dark when it came to a lot of things. I don't know what to think about it anymore. I feel like she kept this big secret from me. One I'll never get to know now that she's gone."

"What was your grandmother's name, sweetheart?" While he thought he knew, he needed her confirmation. Knowing the truth would make everything he needed to tell her easier.

"It was Gwendolen Ambrose. Why do you ask? What does her name have to do with anything?" A realization hit her as soon as she mentioned her grandmother's name. He knew about her, knew her past, and knew her family. She didn't know how he did, but she was going to get to the bottom of it. She would finally get the answers she'd longed for and, just maybe, figure out what her grandmother had been hiding from her.

Gareth, my son, she has revealed the link. You must return to Dinas Emrys immediately and bring her with you. Maelon will soon figure out the truth. When he does, nothing but death will stop him. He will hunt her to the ends of the Earth for as long as he is alive. You have to return to the safety of our home and our clan. The only way to defeat him is for our family to be together. The unity and strength of our clan will be the only thing able to protect her. Gareth heard the desperation in his mother's voice and knew she was right. She didn't use their ability to speak to each other telepathically unless it was an emergency. She wouldn't have reached out to him now unless it was absolutely necessary.

Mam, I'll leave for Wales as soon as I can, but I won't leave without her. She's not ready to take my word for it. I have to convince her to come with me. This won't be an easy task. She doesn't understand anything about her family or the ties that bind them to ours.

The car pulled up in front of her apartment building catching him off guard. He hadn't realized they had gotten there so quickly. Quickly handing the driver the tip he was giving him, he jumped from the car. Yanking her arm, he dragged her out behind him. Quickly scanning the area, he darted up the steps and into her building.

Jerking her arm out of his grasp, she spun to face him. "What the hell is going on? You have exactly five seconds to explain yourself before I call the police." Anger radiated from her body as she paced around the foyer of her apartment building.

"Cadence, please listen. Let's go inside your place, and I promise I'll explain everything." His dragon roared as he sensed the danger surrounding their mate. The beast wanted to be allowed to be called forth. It demanded the right to defend their destiny. "Please, I'm begging you to give me ten minutes."

Spinning, she marched up to her door and unlocked it. Throwing it open, the power of her emotions sent it slamming back into the wall. "If you know what's good for you, you'll start talking."

He followed her into the living room and peeked out the windows. Not seeing anyone or anything out of place, he turned to face her. "Please sit down."

She hesitated before complying and plopping herself down on her couch. She crossed her arms over her chest, and through her gritted teeth she pierced him with her glare. "Start. Talking."

Forcing himself to remain calm, he gently sat down beside her. He faced her and peered into her eyes not knowing where to start. There was so much he needed to tell her, so much he needed her to understand. He knew how farfetched everything would sound and doubted she would give him enough time to fully explain. This wasn't a situation he could sum up in a few words. Frowning, his eyes dropped to his lap.

"Gareth, I'm waiting," she warned tapping her foot. "You're down to eight minutes and don't you think for one second that I'm not completely serious."

"I know you are, but it's hard to explain," he clarified. "I guess the best place to start is your grandmother."

"What does my grandmother have to do with anything?" she snapped, frustrated at his hesitation and his focus on her Nana. "She's dead. None of this, whatever it is, can have anything to do with her."

"Do you know who Merlin is?" he quizzed patiently, thoroughly understanding her aggravation with the situation, and yet finding her temper incredibly sexy.

Gasping at the name, she zeroed in on his face, "Merlin? Seriously, Gareth, what the hell are you talking about? First, you tell me my Nana is involved and now, you're asking about Merlin. I'm starting to think you're crazy." Brow furrowed, she stared at him.

"Cadence, please, just answer my question. I swear to you that it will all make sense."

"Fine. Of course I do, any kid who's ever read about King Arthur knows about the famous wizard." She was seconds away from losing her cool, and anger reared its ugly head. She got that this was an important conversation to him, but the last thing she wanted was to discuss this. She wanted answers, and nothing made sense. He seemed to be caught up in the same delusions as her grandmother.

"His name was Merlin Ambrosius, and his mark, the symbol of his family line, is the one on your pendant. Your grandmother, and, by way of birth, you, are a direct descendant of Merlin." He watched her face for her reaction. He could sense the moment the truth reached her soul.

"But…I thought he was a fictional character. There's no way I'm related to him. This has to all be some kind of weird coincidence. It can't be real," she insisted, even though she knew in her heart that everything he said was true.

Memories of her grandmother came rushing back. All the times she'd said things that didn't make sense. All the things she'd said and done to teach her. All the talk about magic and how the family's magic ran in her veins. She'd never believed a word of it, always believed it was just her grandmother's way of making her sad existence without her parents seem more special.

"I know this seems so out of this world to you, sweetheart, but it explains the talisman that you wear and how you could recognize the language of my ancestors. It will make the next thing I'm going to tell you easier for you to accept."

Seeing the honesty in his eyes, she remembered the bedtime story her grandmother used to tell her. One she'd always thought had been made up, but now suspected was real. "You're a dragon," she gasped.

Chapter Nine

Gareth jerked his gaze up as the realization slipped out of her mouth. He waited for the condemnation, for the fear to forever end what they could have been. He watched as she jumped to her feet and walked around the room. He could feel the emotions rolling off her.

"No, no, no, no," she chanted as she paced. Pausing to look out the window, Cadence fought for composure. When the truth hit her, her past all made sense. She finally understood what her grandmother had been hiding, but it was the bedtime story she used to tell that scared her clear down to the tips of her toes. A fear so deep it felt as if her lungs would explode threatened to overtake her.

"Gareth, am I right? Is everything I used to think was nothing but a fairytale truly my past and my future?" she asked softly.

Going to her, he turned her to face him. "Yes, *un annwyl,* as hard as it is to believe, it's the truth. I would not lie about being a dragon shifter. You are my mate, the one destiny created for me. Surely you can feel the bond building between us, you can feel the pull."

Squeezing the bridge of her nose, Cadence's heart and brain battled each other. Her mind refused to believe what he was claiming, but her heart trusted every word. If she accepted all of the things her grandmother had said over the years as the gospel truth, then she had to consider it as a strong probability that he was being honest with her. Add in her grandmother's witchy items and, as much as she wanted to claim it was all delusional antics, she couldn't.

"The other night, when I heard you speak in my head, it was your dragon speaking to me, wasn't it?"

"Yes, under normal circumstances you wouldn't be able to hear him until the mating ceremony was complete, but the fact that Merlin's blood runs through your veins enhances, our bond. It makes things most people find impossible, a reality." He walked closer as he spoke, trying to gauge her reaction. Wanting to pull her into his arms, he knew it was too soon.

He didn't think they would get as far into the conversation as they had. "I know this is a lot to take in, but we really need to leave. You're in danger. I need to get us back to Dinas Emrys and my clan."

"Why am I in danger? I don't understand." Her eyes widened and her heart raced, as she was reminded of the darkness that surrounded her as she'd walked home the night before. She shivered as the panic resurfaced.

Watching the shadows cross her eyes, he felt her fear. Reaching out he pulled her into his arms, hoping she wouldn't deny him.

Even as the terror tore at her, the comfort she found in his embrace calmed her. It soothed her. As crazy as it sounded, being in his arms felt right, like it was where she was supposed to be.

Sensing when her soul surrendered to him, he tightened his arms around her and she burrowed in deeper. He inhaled her scent and rested his cheek against her head. Her hair was as soft as he'd dreamed it would be.

Listening to the steady beat of his heart, she was conflicted. One part of her needed answers to her questions, the other part of her didn't want to know. The one thing she knew for sure is that she would follow this man to the ends of the earth.

"During the time of King Arthur, Merlin blessed my Red Dragon clan for our undaunted support of him. With his blessing, Merlin transformed us into the first dragon shifters so that we would be able to lead normal lives. It was our brave family, led by my grandfather that defeated the White Dragon invaders from the north. The white dragons spent the last fifteen-hundred years in hiding, preparing for the day they would return."

"A prophecy foretold of a time when the "most revered one," who Merlin blessed, would be born. She would be a descendent of his family; a daughter. She would be the tie that would bind our families together for all eternity. She would be the mate to the heir of the Red Dragon clan and the one who would forever entomb the white dragons." He paused, waiting to see if she figured it out on her own.

"If the heir to the *ddraig wen* is able to kill the girl before the mating ceremony can be completed, then the heir of the red dragons will lose his immortality and his realm. You, my love, are the one the prophecy speaks about, *un annwyl*. You are my mate, my destiny, and the holder of my life."

The feel of her in his arms soothed him and his dragon. Without even trying, she made his world right. Lowering his head, he kissed the top of her hair, inhaling her scent.

Tears ran down her cheeks at the emotion in his voice, and she wished with all that she was that her grandmother had lived long enough to have prepared her for this. "I can't be the one," she whispered into his shirt. "I don't have the ability to stop anyone. Gareth, I don't have the magic in me. Anything magical would have to be my grandmother."

"Destiny isn't wrong, *fy nghalon.* You are everything the prophecy says you are. I can feel the white magic in you. It's there you have just never been taught how to harness it. I can teach you. I can help you learn how to control it. Together we can do anything, and we will defeat the *ddraig wen*, but to do that you're going to have to trust me. Can you do that?"

Inhaling deeply, she stepped back from him and met his gaze. "I know all of this should freak me out and make me seriously doubt your sanity, but it doesn't. Scare me, yes, but I know in my heart that you're telling me the truth. So I guess what I'm saying is yes, I do trust you," she vowed. "Gareth?"

Meeting her eyes, he waited for her to continue.

"Your dragon purrs."

"Dragons do not purr!" he chastised with a smile.

"I'm sorry, but yours does," she responded with a grin as she fought laughter at the look on his face. "Seriously, though, I'll go with you to your family on one condition," she replied with a glint in her eye and a sly smile on her lips.

"If you'll stop accusing my dragon of purring, I'll give you anything. Name your condition," he responded, knowing he'd give her the world if she asked for it. He was already in love with her, would already lay down his life to protect her.

"I want to see your dragon."

Of everything she could have asked for, that wasn't what he'd expected. Smiling for the first time since he'd found her, he shook his head. "I promise when we get back to Dinas Emrys, I'll show you my dragon and anything else you want."

"I do have one other question. Why does the back of my neck burn when you're near?" It had been the one thing that puzzled her the most. It only happened when he was around, so she knew it had to have something to do with him, but she didn't understand how.

"It's the mating mark. It's been there since you were born, but won't be revealed until we complete the mating ceremony. The burning you feel is our bond growing stronger."

Chapter Ten

Maelon Godwin stood in the shadows outside Cadence's apartment, biding his time. Avenging his clan was something he'd been dreaming of for a long time. He'd devised the perfect plan to defeat the Red Dragons and see his beloved white dragons in control of the realm. He'd accounted for every possibility, every counter move Gareth could take, and he was determined to follow his strategy step by step.

If he allowed Gareth to bait him into acting too soon, then he would fail. Using the new blocking trick he'd learned, he cloaked himself. He knew Gareth could sense him when he drew close, and the blocking would give him the advantage he needed. Remaining undetected to Gareth until he was ready, was absolutely crucial to his plan. His new ability would come in handy if he was going to fulfill his family obligation. He had to be the one who finally put them in control of Dinas Emrys.

Steeling himself to the job he had to do, he managed to convince himself that the death of the unknown woman was a necessary evil. It didn't matter whether he personally wanted to kill her or not, in order for him to complete his mission, she had to die. He forced any feelings he might have had about being the one responsible for the death of an innocent to the back of his mind.

Her blood would be on his hands, and he would always feel the taint of it. However, it was something that had to be done, and it had to be by his hand. He was the only one who could take on this vital undertaking. The risk of failure was too great to his family and his future. If he was thwarted, it would be disastrous to his people. He would fail his entire clan, his heritage.

Preparing himself for what his clan's future required of him, he closed his eyes, settling his soul. Focused internally, his mind cleared. Inhaling deeply, he could feel his dragon's calm. His beast centered him and gave him strength. Together as one, they would fulfill their fate. They must face their destiny, united in blood and sealed by death. It was their time to rise up and conquer.

In control, he dropped his mental shield and reached out to Gareth, steeling himself against what he must do. *Enjoy your mate while you can, Gareth. She will not be the one to save you. She will be mine to do with what I wish. She'll beg for death.*

Gareth heard Maelon's challenge in his head, heard the only thing that could shred him. Rage boiled in his blood and his dragon strained against his control. His dragon fought to be released, demanding to be allowed to defend their mate. *You will never touch her! To try guarantees your death,* he vowed, clenching his fists.

"What is it? What's wrong?" Cadence asked, seeing his body language change. Tension rippled through his muscles and his eyes narrowed. It was obvious to her that he was angry. Laying her hand on his arm, she tried to soothe him. "Gareth…"

"We need to go. Come on, sweetheart. I promise it's going to be okay." Taking her hand, he drew her towards the door.

"Wait," she hesitated, jerking her arm from his grasp. "What's going on?" She peered into his eyes and saw distress mixed with fury for the first time. Witnessing the fear in her warrior caused her own terror to build as dread settled in her stomach.

Hugging her to him closely, he ran his fingers through her hair. "I don't want to scare you anymore than I already have. A man named Maelon Godwin is the heir to the white dragon clan, the *ddraig wen*. As the heir, he believes it is his destiny to be the one to personally overthrow the red dragons, essentially me."

"He knows the only way to defeat me is through you. You hold my life, my soul, and my immortality in your hands." Pausing, he slipped his finger under her chin and gently tilted her head back so her eyes would meet his gaze. He was the one who caused the fear he saw etched on her face. If it wasn't for the fact that she was his mate, she wouldn't be in danger.

She was supposed to find love and safety with him, and instead he'd brought danger into her life. The indifference he'd long felt toward the white dragons transformed itself into barely-controlled deadly fury. He would rip every single one of them apart, limb by limb. No one would touch his magnificent beauty.

"Gareth, I don't understand why we need to leave so quickly."

"He's outside on the street right now, sweetheart. We aren't safe here, so we need to leave. The sooner we're back in Wales, the safer I can keep you."

"This makes no sense. What does that have to do with me? You said earlier that I'm the one in danger. If he wants to overthrow you, how does that put me in danger?" Leaning back in his arms, she peered at his face and witnessed the expression he'd tried to hide from her.

"Can we talk about this later, *un annwyl*? We need to go," he all but begged her to let it go for now.

"No, we cannot. We will talk about this now, because I'm not going anywhere until you tell me." Pulling away from him, she backed up and stared him in the eye. Hands on her hips, she planted her feet, refusing to move.

Blowing out his breath in a huff, he began pacing. He didn't want to get into this now, but she wasn't going to let it go. As frustrating as her stubbornness was, he also admired her for it. "Cadence, there is no easy way to say this, but Maelon wants to kill you."

Facing her, he quickly stepped toward her and gently placed his hands on her arms. Running them up and down, he hated the situation he'd put her in. "I swear, I'll protect you with my life. I will not let him get to you. I promise you that I'll keep you safe, but I need you to trust me."

Gasping, terror ran up her spine, "But why? Why does he want to kill me?" Blinking, she fought the tears that were determined to fall.

"It's the ancient prophesy. He knows that if you die before we finish the mating ceremony, I will lose my immortality. Losing that leaves the red dragons vulnerable and more easily defeated. It weakens our people. Once the mating ceremony is complete, my immortality is shared with you, making it much more difficult for them to hurt us and overthrow our people."

Dropping down onto the couch, Cadence hung her head in her hands. Overwhelmed by everything that was happening she struggled to find her composure. It was all so surreal. In less than twenty-four hours, her life had been turned upside down. She wasn't sure which part upset her more. Finding out everything she'd known about her life was a lie, or that someone she'd never heard of wanted her dead.

Kneeling in front of her, he gathered her hands in his. "*Un annwyl*, I won't let him hurt you. I know this is a lot to take in, but we're going to be okay." Kissing the back of her hands, he inhaled her scent. His dragon was on edge, demanding for release. It roared in his head, torn between wanting to protect its mate and wanting to tear Maelon Godwin to pieces. "Cadence…"

"I'm ready." Meeting his gaze, she smiled. Resolved to face her future head-on the way her grandmother had raised her, she was determined to be true to herself. She was never one to bury her head in the sand and pray her problems went away. She would see the danger, come up with a plan, and tackle any obstacle that got in her way. "We're in this together now. Let's show him how strong our bond already is."

Helping her to her feet, he was amazed by her strength and her bravery. Even in the face of danger, she was prepared to stand beside him.

Unable to stop himself he dove towards her, taking her lips with his. Desire poured through him, burning as it flowed. As his lips met hers their tongues tangled, and she matched his passion.

Returning his kiss with equal desperation, Cadence moaned against his mouth. Backing her up against the wall, his lips devoured hers. Pulling her closer, his hard dick fit perfectly between her legs. A moan escaped her lips, bringing him back to the present and the dangerous situation they faced. He broke the kiss having started something they didn't have time to finish. "Let's go," he ordered gruffly.

Chapter Eleven

Pausing before he opened the front door of the apartment building, Gareth dropped his head, leaning it against the door. "I'm sorry," he apologized, blowing his breath out roughly. "I didn't mean to be short with you." Taking his anger out on her had never been his intention. It killed him to think he'd hurt her. *Damn you, Maelon!*

"It's the dragon, isn't it?" she questioned softly, knowing almost instinctively that it was his dragon driving his intense emotions.

"Yes, it senses danger surrounding you… and it's difficult to fight him and you." Stepping back from the door, he rubbed his face with his hands and pushed calm at his dragon. He needed to be able to focus on her and not it. His beast's obstinacy made it difficult.

"Why are you fighting me, Gareth? We're in this together now. This won't work if we're fighting each other."

"I didn't mean it that way, sweetheart. It's not you I'm fighting. I started something with that kiss that I don't have time to finish. Stopping was the hardest thing I've ever done, but with Maelon right outside, making love to you has to wait whether I want it to or not. I have no idea what he has planned, add in my dragon's fury, and I'm twisted emotionally," he responded with a grim smile. "I shouldn't have snapped at you, though, never you!"

Touching the side of his face, she smiled, "It's okay, *un annwyl*. I forgive you."

Meeting her gaze, her love shone bright. "You are amazing. Are you ready?" Leaning down, he kissed her softly, full of promise.

Slipping her hand in his, she nodded her head.

"I need you to follow me and do exactly as I say. I don't know what Maelon will try, but whatever you do, stay behind me. Keeping you safe is all that matters." When she nodded in acknowledgement, he squeezed her hand and slowly opened the door.

As they reached the bottom of the steps, Maelon stepped out of the shadows in front of them. "Hello, Gareth," he goaded. His green eyes were ringed with the fire of his dragon. He stood with his feet apart, poised to attack.

Tucking Cadence in behind him, Gareth met Maelon's glare. "Give it up, Maelon, you aren't going to win," he challenged as he prepared himself for the coming fight. The band around his arm flared to life with his dragon's need for blood.

"There you go again, underestimating me. When are you arrogant Cadells going to learn not to do that? It's only a matter of time before the *ddraig wen* is in control of Dinas Emrys. The only question is, how many of the red dragons will be alive to see it?"

"Seems to me you're the one overreaching here. You will not defeat me, or the red dragons. Your family has already proven their utter failure when it comes to defeating us," he boasted, needing his enemy's anger focused on him and not his mate. Witnessing the crazed look that came over his face, Gareth knew he had succeeded. Growling in rage, Maelon attacked.

Spinning to block the knife glinting in the moonlight, Gareth used his body to protect Cadence. Thrusting his arm, he connected with Maelon's nose, hearing the crack as it broke, and blood poured down his face.

Frenzied in his motions, Maelon dodged to the left, forcing Gareth to step away from Cadence. When the next jab of the knife came, he dodged away, leaving her unprotected.

Hearing her bloodcurdling scream, terror shot through his heart. Whirling around, he watched in horror as a second unnoticed man pulled a knife from her chest.

"No!" he screamed, tearing himself away from his fight and racing to her side. Grabbing her, he pressed his hand to her wound and caught her as her body slumped to the ground. Cradling her in his arms, he screamed as his dragon echoed the anguish in his head.

"The end has come," Maelon taunted. "The *ddraig wen* will have its revenge and its place of honor in Dinas Emrys."

Chapter Twelve

Gathering her into his arms, Gareth sprinted back up the stairs and down the hall to her apartment. Kicking the door open, he raced inside and gently laid her on the couch. He kept his hand pressed tightly against her wound as blood ran between his fingers and pooled on the couch. His dragon snarled, fighting to take control. It roared her name, pushing him closer to the edge.

Mam, help me! Cadence has been stabbed. Please, Mother...I need you! He begged his mother in his mind. *I can't lose her!* Throwing his head back, his scream exploded from him.

Stop! You have to focus. I feel her life force fading. You're almost out of time. Your blood is the only thing that will save her now. You know what to do. It's the only way to save her now!

While his brain knew that was what he had to do, his heart hated it. The moment he gave her his blood, she would gain his immortality, whether she wanted it or not. Unwilling to accept the alternative, he jumped up and ran into the kitchen. Grabbing a knife from the butcher block, he scrambled back to her side. Quickly drawing the blade across his wrist, he lifted her head and brought his bleeding wrist to her mouth.

"Drink, baby, please." His heart felt as if it was breaking into a thousand pieces. For the first time in his life, he didn't care about Dinas Emrys or his immortality. If he lost her, he had nothing left to live for.

He held his breath, silently praying for her to accept his blood. *She's too far gone. Gareth, you have to force it into her. Do it now, before it's too late.* His mother's voice screeched in his head.

Bringing his wrist to his lips, he sucked his blood into his mouth. He leaned over her and pressed his mouth to hers. Using his tongue to force her lips open, he spewed his blood with such force that she automatically swallowed.

Breathing a sigh of relief when he realized she was getting his blood, he ripped open her shirt so he could see the wound. He knew the minute his blood started working. The blood slowed to a drip and the hole in her chest began to heal. Leaning his head down until their foreheads were touching, he kissed her softly. *It's working Mother. The wound is healing.*

She will sleep now. Gareth, get her to the airport; the plane will be waiting to bring you to us. Don't hesitate! Her body needs to heal and you need to be here, where the land strengthens you.

Chapter Thirteen

Pacing outside his childhood bedroom at his parents' home in Dinas Emrys, Gareth ran his fingers through his hair. Frustrated by how long Cadence had been asleep, he struggled to remain calm.

"You can come in now, impatient one," his mother teased.

"You laugh, but I'm scared. What if I did something wrong? What if I didn't give her enough of my blood? Shouldn't she be awake by now?" Sitting down beside the bed, he gathered her hands in his. Reaching up, he stroked her hair back from her face. The dark circles under her eyes seemed lighter somehow.

"You did everything right. Your mate is healing fine. The wound is completely sealed and the scar is almost gone. She will awaken when she's ready."

"He'll be back. He won't stop until she's dead." Bringing her hand to his lips, he kissed it gently. "He will lose this fight. I will not allow him to get close to her again. I failed her once. I will not fail her again."

"This was not your fault. You did everything you could to protect her. You saved her life, and now you both are here in a place where you are protected by our family, our bond, and our strength. He can't touch her as long as the two of you are here." She blocked all emotion from him, not wanting to add to his concerns. While she said the words ensuring their safety, she knew it wasn't the truth. Maelon Godwin and the *ddraig wen* were coming.

The voices around her reeled Cadence back to the present and away from her dreams of her grandmother. She wasn't ready to give up that special time with Nana, but she could hear the suffering in Gareth's voice. Her mate, the man she would spend the rest of eternity with.

"Gareth," she whispered hoarsely.

"I'm here, love." Leaning down towards her, he softly kissed her forehead. Breathing a sigh of relief, he only cared that she was okay. "How are you?"

"What happened? Where am I?" Peering around the room, her eyes came to rest on a beautiful woman standing by his side. An older woman, she had gorgeous red hair and the most stunning green eyes she'd ever seen. It was almost as if they sparkled.

"*Un annwyl*, you're at my family home in Dinas Emrys, in Wales. We were attacked when we left your apartment. Do you remember?" Peering at her closely, he realized she was staring at his mother. "This is my mam, Carys Cadell."

Stepping forward, Carys lay her hand gently on Cadence's leg. "Hello, darling. Welcome to our home. Can I get you anything?"

"No, ma'am, I'm okay, thank you." She couldn't believe she was looking at his mother. *God, I must look a mess. Great first impression, Cadence, you sure know how to make an entrance.*

"Gareth, love, now that you know Cadence is okay. Can you step outside and allow me a minute with her?" Carys asked, giving him the look that advised him that she wasn't asking.

"Mam…"

"Go on, I just need a minute."

Blowing out his breath in a huff, he turned towards the door. "Fine, I'll step outside into the hall, but only for a moment."

Waiting until, he closed the door behind him; Carys faced Cadence and took one of her hands.

"I'm so glad that you're healing up so quickly. I know waking up in a strange land, in a strange bed, surrounded by strange people is nerve racking, my dear. But I want you to know that you're safe here. I had Allen go to your apartment and pack a few bags for you. I figured you might feel a bit more at home with your own things around you."

"Thank you. That was very kind. I admit, this entire situation is a bit much to take in," she responded, fighting to hold onto her composure. "My Nana left a lot of things unsaid. She left a lot of my family history a secret."

"I know, child. Sometimes as we get older, we develop this sense of preservation for our children. I'm sure your Nana had her reasons. I will do everything I can to help you adjust and learn about your past. While he was getting your things together, he found the boxes of your grandmother's things in your living room. I had them send those to us as well. They are all here, ready when you are to go through them."

Knowing her grandmother's things were with her provided Cadence a sense of security. "I can't tell you how much that means to me. Thank you for thinking of that. I really appreciate it."

"You're most welcome." Carys smiled at Cadence torn between needing to comfort the young woman who held the future of her son's life in her delicate hands and the desire to push her to develop her magic so she would be better prepared when the time came. "Gareth, you can come back in."

Rushing into the room, Gareth's eyes took in the two women. Seeing tears on his mate's face instantly angered him. "Mam, what did you say to her? Cadence, are you all right?" He asked as he crossed the room to her side.

"It's okay, Gareth. Your mother didn't say anything wrong. My tears are happy ones. She was kind enough to have my grandmother's things brought to me."

"I'll go start dinner and leave you two alone for a bit," Carys advised as she watched her son's reaction to his mate. Her dragon purred at the love growing between them. Stopping to kiss his cheek, she whispered, "You did well, *un annwyl*."

Sitting down on the edge of the bed beside her, Gareth picked up her hand. "How are you feeling, love?" He leaned down and lifted her hair off her forehead. Peering into her eyes, he watched for any sign of pain.

"I actually feel good. I'm so sorry if I scared you." Squeezing his fingers, she felt tears building.

Opening her eyes wide, she tried to stop them.

"You don't have anything to apologize for. I'm the one who should be apologizing to you," he answered gruffly, remembering how she looked covered in blood and barely alive. He shuddered at the thought as his dragon growled. He gently wiped a tear from her cheek.

"Why would you apologize to me?" she asked, confused as to why he thought he had done anything wrong.

"I failed you! I let Maelon get too close to you. If it hadn't been for me, you wouldn't have been hurt." His anger revealed itself in his voice. Jumping to his feet, he stormed around the room.

"Gareth, stop it right now! You saved my life. If it wasn't for you, I'd be dead!" Watching him in agony, pain tore at her heart. "Or are you Superman, too?"

Spinning around, his eyes met hers and he realized she was teasing him. "Superman, did you really just say that? I can turn into a fierce dragon and all I get is Superman?" He shook his head; she continually amazed him.

"You can turn into a dragon? So you keep saying, but since I've never actually seen it I'm not sure I believe you," she challenged, winking at him.

Throwing back his head, he laughed, "You must be feeling better. Your sarcasm is showing." In two steps he was at her bedside. Reaching out his hand to her, he grinned. "Come on, sassy pants. I'll show you why Superman has nothing on me!"

Chapter Fourteen

Stepping out the back door, Cadence drew in a breath at the landscape before her. "Oh, Gareth, it's beautiful." Looking out over the rolling green, she was amazed at the contrasting feel of Dinas Emrys. "I feel like I've died and gone to heaven."

The noble Dinas Emrys filled all who came upon it with feelings of grandeur of the never-ending hills of lush vegetation. Beneath the exalted crest, Dinas Emrys sat on the ever enduring river, swiftly surging through the Glaslyn River valley. The sumptuous aura that emanated from the solemn vestiges of Llewelyn the Last's glorious castle seeped into her very being. The valiant castle stood just as remarkably as it had in its prime, when it acted as a sentinel to Snowden's mountain pass.

His heart swelled at her love of his home. "You haven't seen anything yet!"

Clasping her hand, he drew her down a path. Winding through the greenest woods she'd ever seen, he paused. "Close your eyes, *un annwyl*."

Doing as he instructed, Cadence closed her eyes and allowed him to lead her. She felt his hands on her arms when he stepped up behind her, and his breath tickled the back of her neck.

"Open your eyes, love," he whispered.

Taking a moment, Cadence focused on the air around her. The light breeze tickled her cheeks, and the scent of the flowers flooded her nose. Opening her eyes, the first thing she saw was the beautiful waterfall from her dreams.

Awestruck, with no words to properly express her enthrallment, she couldn't pull her eyes away from the little utopia hidden away from the prying eyes of most. A clandestine paradise saved only for the worthy. Chaste in nature, its ornate modesty made the perfect contradiction. A crystalline canopy of water cascaded down an altar of radiantly shining stones, into a natural rock pond. The rippling lake beneath the captivating waterfall, rushed against the endless garden of evergreen earth encompassing it. It was a grotto filled with the gentle tears of dragons past; clean and pure.

"Oh, it's so incredibly beautiful. Gareth, I've had dreams of this place. How it is possible?" Cadence's eyes soaked up all the beauty surrounding her. From the gorgeous view to the scents and feeling in the air, everything touched her heart and soul.

"I'm not sure, sweetheart, unless it's your magic that is making it happen. This is a holy place for the dragons and one of your people as well. It's only natural that you would be drawn to it."

"It's amazing. I can't believe my Nana never told me about our family. The stories, love, and ancestry we could have shared would have been wonderful. To think she felt like she had to keep it from me breaks my heart."

"I don't know why she kept it from you, love. But I'm sure she had her reasons. Rest assured, she knows how you feel now and she's enjoying it with you. Now, enough with the sadness are you ready for your surprise?" he asked cheekily. Seeing her nod, he kissed her forehead. "Wait here," he ordered as he walked out into the middle of the clearing.

One minute the love of her life stood proudly before her, then right before her eyes, he faded away and a large dragon stood before her. Soaking up every inch of him, his dragon was even more glorious than she had expected... not that she was exactly sure what to expect, having never seen a dragon in person before.

Standing four stories tall, the noble crimson dragon stretched and spread his magnificent wings wide. His wing span was so large that they almost touched the trees on the sides of the clearing. Luminous gold plates covered his chest like a suit of shimmering armor.

The golden scales on his chest were flanked by innumerable scarlet plates. They protected the mighty beast's heart from anything that would attack him. Hard as diamonds, nothing could penetrate them.

His honey amber eyes glowed with warmth that didn't seem possible for the mighty beast. She had expected dead, haunting eyes and not ones filled with love. They betrayed the fierce fighter that he was.

His long snout was topped with a horn that arched back towards his face. The point was sharp and able to tear something in two with the flick of his chin. Two more razor-sharp horns ran from his eyes and along the top of his head. They stretched back behind him protecting him from an attack from behind.

Large barbs, colored a deep golden brown, followed along the curve of his spine. His golden-ringed tail lay wrapped around his body, its spiked end, a weapon of death.

She approached him slowly, soaking up all his glory. Fascinated by his size and his beauty, she felt driven to lay her hands upon him. Knowing he'd never hurt her, any hesitation and fear at his frightening looks vanished with her knowledge that he loved her.

When she neared he slowly lowered his head, and she reached out to touch the side of his face. Running her hand down his head, she savored the strength that poured off him. Terrifying abilities and powerful strength emanated from him. Had she not known the man inside the dragon, she would never have approached this formidable beast.

Pivoting, she walked the length of him, inspecting every inch of his side. She trailed her fingers along his plates, relishing the feel of his rock-hard scales. Slipping her fingers under the scales, she could feel the softness of his flesh. Returning to his lowered head, she stepped up on her tip toes to plant a kiss on his cheek. "You're absolutely breathtaking," she whispered. "I love both of you!"

He nudged her back with his nose and waited until she was far enough away from him to change safely. As he returned to his human form, the heat from his eyes burned and ignited the flames inside her. His passion-filled gaze never left hers as he approached.

Desire swept through her as he neared, her blood boiling with need. Circling her, he conducted his own inspection, touching every inch of her arms. Softly, like a feather along her skin, his fingertips savored the smoothness of her. His nostrils took in the scent of her desire, and his heart beat wildly at the love coming from her.

Stopping in front of her, he swung her up into his arms. Taking her lips with his, he made his way to the edge of the water. Laying her down on a bed of moss, he devoured her mouth. Trailing kisses along her jaw, he suckled and nipped his way down her neck. Ripping open her blouse, his eyes took in her naked beauty. Rose-colored nipples begged to be feasted upon. Lowering his head, his tongue circled her peak.

Closer and closer to her nipple, she moaned for more.

"What, love," he whispered, "tell me what you want." Snaking his hand down her stomach, he slipped it underneath the waist of her jeans.

"Gareth, please, I'm burning up," she begged, as her hips jerked closer to his hand.

In one fluid move, he ripped her jeans off. His breath caught as he realized she didn't have anything on underneath. Finding her naked from the waist down, he couldn't wait another second to taste her. Sliding down her body, he kissed and licked his way across her abdomen.

As he neared her core, he scented her desire. Her unique aroma teased his dragon. Resisting his dragon's desire to take her, he took his time. Her hips thrust forward and her body contracted with need.

Lowering his head, he drew his tongue up her center, savoring her flavor. It burst into his mouth as he plunged his tongue into her. Throwing his arm over her stomach, he held her in place as he consumed her nectar. Swirling his tongue around her clit, he slipped his finger into her. He felt her walls constrict as her orgasm began to build.

As he gently bit down on her clit, her body shook and she exploded. Eyes narrowed with lust, he licked and suckled until her body relaxed in the aftermath of her release. Raising himself over her, the moment she exhaled he rammed into her, reigniting the flames of passion.

He couldn't take his eyes off her face as he fought to hold onto his composure. His dragon urged him higher. Driving into her, he buried himself deeply into her as his own release shot through him.

Falling to the side, he rolled onto his back, pulling her body with him. Cradling her in his arms, his heart beat rapidly and he reveled in the strength of their mating bond. He cherished his mate, "*Ydych yn fy nghalon, fy enaid, fy mywyd,*" he whispered. "You are my heart, my soul, and my life, Cadence."

Chapter Fifteen

Basking in the glorious love growing between him and his mate, his mind erupted with his mother's screams. Bolting to his feet, he swiftly threw on his jeans. "Hurry, *un annwyl*. We must return. My mother is in danger." His dragon roared in his head when Maelon's voice howled in fury.

"No!" he screamed as the vision of a knife plunging into his father's throat bombarded his mind. The pain was almost enough to drop him to his knees. Clutching her hand, he ran towards his home. He pushed himself faster, silently begging her to keep up. The mark on his arm burned, and he knew he had to let his dragon free. Abruptly coming to a stop, he faced her. "Cadence, I have to let my dragon take over. My family is being attacked. You have to stay here where it's safe. Please, don't follow me. Stay here until I return."

Nodding, Cadence didn't dare speak. Fear for him and his family overwhelmed her, and she followed his orders. The rocky outcropping provided the perfect cover for her. It created a small cave that she could curl herself up in without being seen, until he could return.

Kissing her roughly, he tore himself away and took off at a run. When there was enough space between them, he transformed into his fierce dragon. His majestic wings unfurled, flapping furiously as he took flight. He disappeared in a blink of an eye, and Cadence silently began praying.

She chanted a safety protection spell she remembered from her youth. She didn't know if she did it right, or if it would even work. She also had her doubts that there was anything magical about her. But she had to do something to help. She couldn't sit back and do nothing, and just in case he was right about her family she would use the magic for something good.

The love she held for him and his family members made the possibility of something happening to one of them caused fear to rip through her heart. Even though she hadn't really gotten to know them, they had been there for her, cared for her, and helped her heal. There was nothing in this world she wouldn't do for them. She knew it would be too much to bear if he didn't get to them in time. She would forever blame herself for their deaths.

Diving towards the ground, Gareth could see two dragons locked in fierce battle. Forcing his wings to go faster, he approached the two beasts. They would fight to the death, neither one of them willing to back off. He couldn't allow his brother to fight his battles. He tried to reach them before the death blow could be delivered, but he was too late. Just as he reached the two dragons, he watched his brother kill the other dragon.

The bloody and dirty red dragon of his brother broke away from the downed white dragon, signaling an end to the fight. Gareth quickly resumed his human form the moment his feet touched the earth and watched as his brother changed back too.

"Are you okay?" he asked his brother as he tried to determine where the blood came from.

"Just some scratches," Luc Cadell replied, wiping a blood smear across his forehead. "Maybe a few stitches, but nothing Mother can't handle. I'm going to make sure that son of a bitch is gone."

Knowing his brother was in one piece and not seriously injured, he nodded at him as he transformed and flew away. He knew Luc could handle anything and would alert him if trouble was still on their lands. He turned and raced to where his mother sat on the ground with his father's crumpled body in her lap. With her hands pressed to his throat, she had her eyes closed as she prayed for his life.

Dropping to his knee beside the prone form of his father, his heart shattered at seeing the strong man broken and bloody. It was a sight he'd never expected to see and one he didn't ever want to see again. "What the hell happened?" he growled as he watched the tears stream down his mother's face. She wasn't a crier. She was the one who held it all together when things got rough or someone was injured. Seeing the emotional reaction from his mother made him all the more determined to take out Maelon Godwin.

"Where's Luc?" she asked as she looked for her other son. "Is he okay?"

"He's fine; some scrapes, and he may need to be stitched up, but he said it wasn't anything you hadn't seen before. He flew out to check the perimeter to make sure Maelon isn't still lurking around. He'll be here shortly. Now, tell me what happened."

"Maelon and Ian Godwin came out of nowhere, Gareth. One minute your father and I were sitting on the patio enjoying the weather and the next Maelon was there, attacking your father. Both of the Godwin's were circling your father when Luc showed up. That's when Ian Godwin attacked your brother."

"It was utter chaos. There wasn't anything I could do to help. They were locked in battle and before

I realized what was happening, your father collapsed on the ground and Maelon took off. The bloody coward didn't even stay to help his brother." Her body shook as she held her seriously injured husband. His blood ran hot and sticky between her fingers, onto the ground.

"They shouldn't have been able to attack us here. We should have known they were near. How did they do this, Gareth? I don't understand."

"I don't understand it either, but I *will* get to the bottom of this. Maelon will pay for what he has done. I swear to you he will. Mam is Father going to be okay?" he asked hesitantly, scared by the amount of blood and afraid his father was going to die.

"Yes, he will survive this. His life force is healing his body already. In a few hours, he'll be awake and cranky." She paused, staring at her blood-covered hands. "He's stronger than Maelon gave him credit for. It takes more than one wound to kill a Cadell. Maelon was sloppy. The attack doesn't make any sense…" Panic filled her as she realized Cadence was missing. "Gareth, where is Cadence?"

"I left her at the outcropping, where she was safe." The minute he said it, he knew he'd made a mistake. "He attacked to draw me out. Damn it, I left her unprotected." Hearing the flapping of wings, he turned as his brother, Luc, landed and transformed into his human form.

"Where is that son of a bitch?" he growled as he raced towards them.

"Don't worry about that now! Go!" Carys yelled at her sons. "You must save Cadence and get to her before he does!"

Chapter Sixteen

Taking off in the direction of her hiding place, Gareth and Luc sprinted towards Cadence. "You left her alone again? What were you thinking?" Luc asked, angry at his brother's misjudgment.

"Shut up, Luc. At the time I didn't know what I was flying into, and I refused to expose her to danger again." Gareth was beating himself up for not realizing what Maelon had been up to, but his dragon echoed his brother's sentiments. "I didn't stop to think that it was a trick. All I saw was Father being attacked and I had to get there quickly. I couldn't do that in human form."

"When are you going to learn that until you complete the mating bond, you can't leave her alone, ever? She must always have someone with her! It's the only way to guarantee her safety," Luc chastised. "You aren't this stupid. Why the hell weren't you anticipating what those bastards would do?"

"I was focused on saving your ass and getting to Father. Damn it, Luc! How the hell did Maelon get past the wards we put up? How is he blocking us? Neither of those things should have been possible. Dragons don't have cloaking powers."

Arriving at the outcropping, Gareth's eyes raked in his

surroundings as he screamed for her. "Cadence!" He didn't see anything out of place, but that didn't mean anything. "Do you sense anything?"

"No," Luc replied. "But I didn't sense them earlier either." Reaching out with all of his senses, he tried to pinpoint if Maelon was there. Frustration surged through him as he fought the urge to punch something. *Where the hell are you, Maelon? Show yourself you bastard!*

Crawling out of her hiding place, Cadence's eyes met Gareth's. Pain and anguish were reflected in them, along with fear. "Gareth, I'm here."

Rushing to her, he wrapped her tightly in his arms, "I was afraid he had gotten to you!"

Relief flooded his body when his arms closed around her. Squeezing her firmly, he thanked the Gods she was safe. Able to relax slightly, he forced feelings of peace at his dragon. He felt it slowly calm with her presence. "I'm so sorry I left you again. Can you forgive me?"

Leaning back in his arms, she peered up into his haunted eyes. Laying her hand on his cheek, she smiled. "I'm fine... nothing happened to me. See? I'm in one piece, just the way I was when you left. Please tell me your family is okay."

Kissing her softly on the forehead, love and admiration rushed through him. Every moment, she continued to amaze him. She was able to take everything in stride, every crazy event, every crazy thought. Throughout all that had happened, she continued to stand by him. It filled him with pride at her strength and determination. The thought that she could have been hurt or worse because of his actions killed him. Her arms tightened around him when she felt him tense.

Shaking off the foreboding and negative thoughts, he refused to scare her any more. "They'll be okay. My father was injured but Mother is with him." Releasing her, he took her hand in his. "Cadence, I want you to meet someone. This is my brother, Luc. Luc, this is Cadence, my soul mate and the love of my life."

Hearing Gareth's words, Cadence blushed like a school girl. She smiled as she turned to the man standing behind him. Extending her hand, she greeted him. "Luc, it's lovely to meet you."

Ignoring her outstretched hand he pulled her into a bear hug, squeezing her tightly. "I can't believe you love that big lug," he teased as he set her down. "Are you sure you're not just hanging out with him out of pity?"

She playfully batted at his arm, "No, it's not a pity date," she giggled. "I really do love this grumpy old dragon."

Grinning at her, Luc already loved his soon-to-be sister. He'd felt her magic as well as her goodness when she'd been hurt. He'd seen firsthand how she affected his brother, and he loved her all the more when he saw that she felt the same way about his sibling. Hearing the concern in her voice for his father and their family sealed the deal for him. Throw in a wicked sense of humor and she fit right in with their family.

"We need to get back to the house and see how we can help Mother," Gareth advised. Pulling Cadence beside him, he led the way towards their home. Luc stayed a step behind them to protect their backs.

"Your brother looks just like you, only not as serious," she teased.

Snorting, he glanced back at Luc. "He's a pain in my ass," he grumbled, knowing his brother could hear every word.

"But you still love me," Luc challenged.

"So you say," Gareth retorted, punching his brother in the arm.

"Ouch, why did you do that? You know I'm a mighty warrior who just got injured in battle. Be gentle!" he ordered as he pouted.

"Give it a rest! You barely have a scratch. You're just trying to get sympathy from Cadence!" As they neared the house, Gareth spied the fallen dragon. It had returned to its human form in death. Where the dragon once lay, in its place was the dead body on Maelon Godwin's brother, Ian.

"We need to dispose of the body. Leaving it there isn't right," Gareth said, believing that even though the Godwin had attacked them in their home, he still deserved a decent burial.

"They wouldn't do that for us," Luc challenged. "They would leave our bodies to rot where they fell."

"That's what separates us from them. We will do right by him. It's how our clan operates. We will not allow them to turn us into someone we aren't. We will not lower ourselves because it's what they would do. Our parents would want more from us as would our clan." He knew that to dishonor the fallen Godwin was to dishonor their family, their code and their ancestors.

"Luc, Gareth is right. Leaving him to lie there isn't what good people do. We need to treat him as we would want our family treated," Cadence agreed. Gently touching his arm, she wished she knew how to comfort him. It was obvious to her that he was struggling with the anger he felt towards the Godwin's. She understood the anger, and knew that Gareth felt the same rage.

Glancing back and forth between the two of them, Luc knew in his heart they were right. He knew it was what his father would want them to do, but he couldn't help but feel angry. They had attacked them in their home. They'd attacked Cadence and Gareth, and now his parents. It was only a matter of time before they attacked again. Kicking at the grass like a petulant child, he shrugged his shoulders. "You're both right, but that doesn't mean I have to like it. I'll find kindling." Stalking off, he went looking for the wood they would need.

"Kindling, I don't understand. What is that for?" Cadence asked in confusion.

"A bonfire is the only true way to honor a fallen dragon. We were forged in fire, thus upon death we return to the fire. It's how we pay tribute to our dead. Some say that if a dragon is not returned to the fire and earth, they can never reach the heavens.

Their souls will be damned to walk the Earth forever."

"That's awful. We can't let that happen. I know what they've done, but we have to do the right thing."

Leaning down to kiss the top of her nose, Gareth treasured her gentle soul. "And so we will, my love. We'll take care of it right now," he reassured her, pointing at where Luc returned dragging a large log.

Taking turns cutting up the log, Gareth and Luc worked silently to build a pyre. Once it was finished, they lifted Ian Godwin, positioning him on top of the pyre. Saying a silent prayer for peace, Gareth held a lit torch to the kindling and stood back to watch as it ignited.

They stayed at the fire, keeping watch on the young man's body. Leaving him didn't seem right to any of them. Even in death, they didn't want him to be alone. The concern for their father urged them to leave, but they knew their father would live and he would want them to watch over Ian Godwin.

"Maelon will be out for blood," Luc stated as he watched the firelight flicker into the night. "He'll want vengeance for Ian. He'll want my death as payment."

"That's not happening. He can want vengeance all he wants, Luc. He won't get it. They came onto our lands and attacked our home. We had every right to defend ourselves. He came looking for a fight he couldn't win, and his brother paid the price. Ian's blood is on his hands. If he steps foot on our lands again, I'll send him to keep his brother company," Gareth swore. He jerked his head up searching the area for Maelon when he heard his voice echo in his mind.

Your brother took something that I loved. He owes a death debt to me now. I'll be coming to collect it when I come for your beloved mate. Maelon stood under the cover of the trees shaking in his rage. His brother's death would be avenged. He would make sure his brother wasn't the only dragon laid upon a pyre.

If it was the last thing he did, Gareth Cadell would follow

his brother into the heavens and so would any other Cadell who got in his way. They would pay for Ian's death in Cadell blood and their lands.

Clenching his fists, Gareth felt hatred steamrolling through his blood and igniting his dragon's wrath. *Luc owes you nothing. You attacked on our lands. I'm sorry about Ian but he shouldn't have been here. Neither one of you should have been here. I promise you Maelon, try it again and you will join your brother in the heavens.*

As he watched his brother, Luc could sense Maelon even though he couldn't hear him. "What is he saying?"

"Just more of his threats nothing we can't handle," Gareth

advised his brother, not really wanting to have this conversation in front of Cadence.

"How is he blocking us? He shouldn't have that ability," Luc asked, worried by the whole situation. "As long as he can shield himself from us, he has the advantage."

"We'll figure it out. We always do. The Godwin's haven't beaten the red dragons ever and I'm not about to let them start now. Right this minute, though, we need to get back to the house and check on our father." Grabbing Cadence's hand, he headed towards their home.

Chapter Seventeen

Arriving at the family home, Gareth escorted Cadence inside while Luc scouted the area, looking for any sign of Maelon. In the kitchen, his mother sat sipping a cup of tea, and her eyes met theirs as they made their way towards the table. "He's resting. He'll be as good as new before you know it," she answered his unspoken question. "Cadence, darling, are you okay?"

Rushing to her side, Cadence laid her hand on Carys' arm. "I'm fine, how are you?" Knowing what she had been through, she worried about Gareth's mother.

"I'm fine, child. It takes more than one *ddraig wen* to bring my Emery down. Did you take care of Ian Godwin?"

"Yes, we did. We gave him the burial he should have had, even though he didn't deserve it," Luc muttered.

"Everyone deserves an honorable burial, my son. He was following the desires of his family. You can't fault him for that."

"Mam, he attacked Gareth. He attacked Cadence, and then he attacked Father. How can I not find fault in his actions?" Luc challenged, feeling as if his mother had sympathy she shouldn't.

"Would you have done any differently if Gareth had asked you to fight for him? Would you have backed up your family whether or not you believed in what they were fighting for? Or would you have walked away and let them fight their battles alone?" Carys asked of her youngest son.

"You know I would never walk away from any fight my family was in. I would back them up with everything I had."

"Then you do understand Ian Godwin's stance. All it takes is a bit of understanding and compassion to make even the staunchest of enemies more human to you. Regardless of whether or not we agree with the path the Godwin's are on right now, their family has the same loyalty and ties that our own has. That deserves to be honored." Walking up to her youngest, she patted his cheek. "Now, enough of this, what's done is done. We move on to the next problem. Cadence, there is one thing I need you to do for me."

"I'll do anything, Mrs. Cadell," Cadence swore. Gareth's family had welcomed her with open arms, and would soon be her family as well. She would deny them nothing.

"Please, call me Carys or Mam, whichever is more comfortable to you. I do have a big favor to ask of you, so please, think about it before you answer." With a nod of her head, Carys continued. "We need to perform the mating ceremony as soon as possible. I know you love my son as much as he loves you. I know this is happening quicker than you probably expected, but until we do, you and Gareth are in grave danger. The mating will protect you both."

Cadence didn't think her heart could hold any more love, but she'd been wrong. The moment Carys uttered her favor, Cadence knew she was exactly where she needed to be and with the family she was meant to join. "Nothing would make me happier than to begin the mating ceremony right now. I love him with all of my being and I love all of you as well. I've waited all my life for him." Tears ran down her cheeks as everything she'd ever dreamed of became her reality. She felt her grandmother instantly, and suddenly understood everything she'd ever said.

"You don't have to do this, Cadence. We will wait and do it right. Mam, you had no right to ask such a thing from her. We've already turned her world upside down. Mating is eternal and not a decision to make lightly," Gareth spit out. He'd already exposed her to danger twice. He wasn't about to take away anything else. She deserved for them to handle the mating ceremony the right way. She deserved to stand before him and know that they were mating because of the incredible love between them. To pledge her life to him because it was what destiny intended, not because she felt pressured because of a family feud with the Godwin's. *This is about her, not the family legacy.*

"Gareth, I love you even more that you are willing to wait. I really do, but your family is in danger. If the mating ceremony can remove some of the danger, then I don't need more time. I know exactly how I want to spend eternity, and that is by your side. I've finally found my soul mate, my other half. That's all I really need to know. I don't want to wait, either. I want to join our lives as soon as possible," she said as tears of joy ran down her face. She loved that he wanted to protect her. She loved that he wanted to make everything perfect for her. "If the mating ceremony means I'm going to spend eternity with you, then let's get mated!"

"Are you sure, *un annwyl*? I don't want you to have any regrets." His eyes searched hers for any doubt. He looked for any sign she wasn't as sure as she claimed. "Eternity is a long time sweetheart. I want you to be absolutely sure."

"No regrets, Gareth. I want a long life with you, full of love and family. I already know exactly what I want and I don't want to wait anymore than your mother does."

"Cadence, walk with me a minute," he asked, extending his hand. "We'll be back shortly."

Taking Gareth's hand, Cadence followed him out to the back yard.

Chapter Eighteen

Stepping out into the yard, Gareth's eyes were immediately drawn to the smoldering pyre. As much as he wanted to hate the Godwin's, he still felt a grieving ache at the loss of life. Ian Godwin was a good man and he didn't deserve to die. "Cadence, this is a serious matter. Lives are being taken and lines are being drawn. I hate that you have been drug into the middle of a bloody war. You life doesn't have to be altered further by being forced into mating with me to soon."

"My life has already been changed and nothing can undo that. You knew once we met, the mating bond would dictate where our lives would go. Why are you questioning it now? I thought you wanted to be mated to me."

Running his fingers through his hair, he signed in frustration. "It's not that I don't want to be mated to you," he all but growled. "You know that I do and that I love you beyond words, but…"

"No buts, you love me and I love you. Our mating is inevitable and destined, waiting doesn't make any sense." Growing aggravated at his obstinance, she wanted to smack him. "Why are you being so difficult?"

"I'm not trying to be difficult. I'm trying to be considerate and do what is best for you." He replied, starting to get annoyed. "You're the one who doesn't understand."

"Understand, seriously Gareth, did you just say that? I understand perfectly. I am standing right here, ready to defend you and your family and ready to take on anyone who gets in our way. I've accepted we're mates and that our lives are destined to be intertwined. I've accepted that our futures are inescapably linked to our mating. What I know is that I finally found the love of my life and a family that wants me and he's asking me to not go through with the mating ceremony. How do you think that makes me feel?" She yelled as tears ran down her face. Hurt and anger boiled up inside of her at his rejection.

"I want the mating ceremony, Cadence. I want you mated to me more than I want to draw my next breath. I need you more than anything I've ever needed. Please, *un annwyl*, never doubt my feelings for you." Hating himself for the tears he'd caused, he reached out and stroked her cheek. "You are my everything and I simply wanted to ensure that you were mating with me because it was your choice and not my mother's."

"It is, Gareth. I don't know how to make you believe that I want this. You mother just made it happening quickly a reality. I swear to you that if I wasn't ready I would tell you that. I'm not a wallflower, love. I am a grown woman with my own opinions. I've never let anyone make me do something I didn't want to do and I'm not about to start now."

"Then it's settled, we're getting mated." He smiled, trying to hide the doubts he still had. He didn't doubt her love, just her motivations behind doing it quickly.

"I just wish my Nana…Oh my God…Gareth, my Nana." Realization dawned on her and she couldn't believe she'd missed the obvious.

"What about her?"

"I don't know why I didn't think of this before. Didn't you say that dragons don't have cloaking abilities?" She asked excitedly, finally feeling like she would be able to help him.

"Yes, but what does that have to do with you Nana?" Confused by her change of subject, he couldn't figure out where she was going.

"I have all of her things, her *magical* things. If cloaking isn't something dragons can do naturally, then it's something Maelon *learned* to do. Normal people can't cloak either so it had to be a magical being who taught him. What do you want to bet that there is something in her books on cloaking?"

Grinning, he picked her up and swung her around. "You my love are brilliant!!!" Planting a kiss on her lips, he thanked the Gods for leading him to her. "We need to get your things to Dinas Emery."

"Your mother is a step ahead of you. She arranged for Alan to send them here. I have all of Nana's things in my room."

"That's my mother! We may finally have an advantage. Thank you, sweetheart!"

"All we need to do now is go through all of her things. I just know there has to be something in one of her books on cloaking." Cadence beamed with pride that she was finally able to feel like she was contributing to her new family's fight with the white dragons. She didn't like being the one who needed constant protection. Now, not only would she be able to connect with her grandmother even more, she just might be able to figure out how to use the magic running through her blood.

"We will read everything she left you, after the mating. Right now, the only thing I want to focus on is securing our future together. The White Dragons can wait."

"Gareth, are you sure? What if they come after us again?" Fear twisted in her stomach at the thought that they could be attacked at any time.

Touching her cheek, her concern for his family made him love her even more. "We don't have to worry yet, sweetheart. With the death of Ian, they will mourn him first. When a dragon dies, the clan will grieve for a month before they will plan their revenge. We have time now."

Chapter Nineteen

Standing in the bedroom, Cadence admired the gown Carys found for her to wear. It was the most gorgeous dress she'd ever seen. The golden chiffon sheath had an illusion boatneck and was decorated with lace appliqués. The skirt flowed around her feet giving it an ethereal feel. At the waist, a vibrant red sash encircled her glowing form. It was perfect for her to wear when she married her red dragon.

Twirling in front of the mirror, she fell in love with the way the skirt swirled around her legs. Slipping her feet into red satin ballet shoes, she felt like a princess. Hearing a gasp behind her, she spun around and saw Carys standing in the doorway.

"You look absolutely beautiful, Cadence." Carys couldn't stop the tears of joy from slipping out. Pulling a tissue from her pocket, she dabbed her eyes. "You will bring so much love and joy to my son and our family. I've always wanted a daughter and now I have you."

"Carys, thank you so much for this amazing dress. I never imagined that I'd wear something as delicate and glamorous as this."

"It fits you perfectly. You will be my son's dream come true. Thank you for agreeing to do this for us. I know it's probably not how you envisioned your wedding day, but I wouldn't have asked you if it wasn't important."

"I'm as excited as you are. I don't need to wait. Gareth is the one for me and I can't wait to seal our life together. The only thing I would change is that my grandmother could be here with me, but you have all welcomed me into your family. Having you with me is all I need."

She allowed herself to be drawn into a hug, cherishing the woman who would become her mother.

"No matter what happens in the future, we will always protect you. We will always be here for you. Your safety is as important to me, as my son's."

Stepping out of the hug, Cadence faced her. "I know that, and I hope you know that I will do everything I can to protect you all as well. You're my family now, and that's extremely important to me."

"Before the ceremony, I want to give something to you. It's been in our family for years and I'm passing it down to you." Holding out a small box, Carys' heart constricted with love for Cadence. "I never had any daughters of my own. Yet the Gods blessed me with a daughter in you. I promise you that I will always hold you with the same love and devotion as I do my sons."

Opening the small box, Cadence stared at the jeweled pin with awe. "I love it. It's beautiful. Is that a dragon scale?"

"Yes, my dear. When Owain Cadell became the first dragon shifter, he was a fierce warrior. In a battle against the Godwin's, one of his scarlet plates was damaged and this small piece was broken off. A woman names Elena found it and saved it for him. Later, after the war ended, she took it to Owain and gave it back to him. They fell in love and eventually married."

"On the day of their marriage, he presented her with this jeweled pin he'd had made from the plate she'd returned to him. He gave it to her as a sign of his eternal love and devotion. Every wife of the red dragon heir has carried this pin. It has been passed down in the generations since, as a sign of the loyalty and love we hold for our husbands. Their lives are full of strife and the trials of ruling the clan."

"It's not an easy job and they need the support of their wives. This fragile piece of Owain's scale represents how fleeting life can be. It reminds us that love and family are the only things that matter in this world. As the woman who is pledging to love and honor my son for all eternity, this now belongs to you. My mother gave it to me when I mated with Emery, and now I'm giving it to you."

Tears spilled from Cadence's eyes as she listened to the story of Owain and Elena. "Thank you so much. I will cherish this always."

Helping her attach the pin to her dress, Carys smiled as her heart exploded with love. "Are you ready for your destiny?"

Wrapping her arms around her soon-to-be mother's neck, Cadence didn't even try to hide the tears. "I'm more than ready!" she exclaimed hugging her tightly.

Dabbing at her tears so she didn't smear her make-up, Carys kissed her cheek. "Then let's go. My son is waiting for you."

Chapter Twenty

Standing in front of the crystal blue waterfall, Cadence felt the serenity of her own personal paradise in the very core of her being. The mist of the water sparkled as the sunlight penetrated it. Clouds opened up to reveal the gorgeous sky behind them. The beauty surrounded her soul and made her feel as if she'd finally come home.

Looking out over the water, she could see her grandmother standing by an out-cropping of rocks. Her grandmother's love caressed her, reassuring her of her family's love. Her Nana's hand waved in farewell as she slowly faded. Cadence could feel the gentle kiss on her cheek.

As the sunlight broke through a cloud, it illuminated where she stood, surrounding her in its warm glow.

Fragrant flowers saturated the air with their sweet scent.

Hearing a gasp, her eyes drew upward to meet the beautiful amber eyes of her soul mate. His eyes reflected the love and devotion he felt for her.

"You look stunning," Gareth whispered as his eyes soaked up the sight of her. His heart swelled when he stepped forward, taking her hands in his. His dragon preened for its mate.

Smiling at the man she would spend the rest of her life with, the weight of the responsibility suddenly weighed her down. Glancing around, she met the curious eyes of Gareth's clansmen. She could feel their scrutiny, their doubts, but more importantly she could feel their hope. Hope for the future. Hope for the continuity of the Red Dragon clan.

Never in her wildest dreams did she expect to find a love so pure and powerful with her soul mate. It was a love that she'd thought lived in fairy tales. Dressed in the long, flowing golden gown, she felt like a princess.

Meeting Gareth's gaze, Cadence felt her heart pounding with excitement. His dragon's essence swirled around her, soothing her nerves. The butterflies wreaking havoc in her stomach settled. In his eyes, she witnessed the love she felt for him reflected back at her.

She knew in her heart he didn't want their mating to be rushed the way it had. But she didn't care how it came about. The only thing that mattered to her was being mated to the incredible man standing before her. She had no doubts about their love and devotion to each other.

Peering into her eyes, Gareth's heart was torn. He wanted to be mated to his raven-haired princess. He needed to complete the bond with her like he needed his next breath. She was his very heartbeat, his life. He loved her more than he ever thought possible, and yet it felt wrong.

The ceremony felt forced by the white dragons and Maelon Godwin. He wanted more for her. He wanted their mating to occur because of love, and not out of necessity and clan responsibility. But she refused to listen. She was determined to give in to his mother's demands and complete the mating ritual now.

Gareth, she loves you. His mother's voice echoed in his head. *She wouldn't have agreed to this if she didn't. You know that, and I know it, let it go. Complete the ceremony and spend the rest of your long life loving her.* He could almost feel the mental head slap she was giving him.

Seeing the pin attached to her gown, his breath caught. He knew what it represented, but he also knew what the pin meant to his mother. It was her most prized possession.

While he knew it was tradition for the mother to pass the pin on to the bride of the next dragon heir on their mating day, he never really thought his mother would part with the pin as long as his father was still alive.

His heart lurched at the symbolism in his mother's gift. He vowed then to never take her gift for granted. He would always put Cadence first, above all else. If she was happy about the mating, then he wouldn't question it. He wouldn't tarnish their day with his doubts. Most importantly, he would spend the rest of his life making sure she never regretted her life with him and never doubted his love for her.

Carys Cadell wore her finest red robe with golden trim. It floated around her feet as if she walked on a crimson cloud. Her eyes misted with unshed tears as she studied the couple before her, the future of her clan, and the future of her family.

Taking slow steps towards Gareth and Cadence, she eased Merlin's sacred athame from its golden sheath. She ran her finger reverently along its razor-sharp blade. His pure white magic hummed around her and sent electrical pulses up her arm. She could sense his strong force taking over the area.

Reaching out, she took Gareth's strong hand in hers. She drew the athame across his palm and a thin
line of blood erupted from his skin. Turning, she gingerly accepted Cadence's delicate hand and sliced her palm as well. Joining their bloodied palms, she gingerly entwined them with an old flaxen rope that once belonged to Merlin. The minute the circle was complete; their hands began to vibrate with Merlin's fierce white magic. It traveled through their bodies, burning the united blood in their veins.

Facing the couple, Carys met their gazes. "Today we celebrate the intertwining of these two souls, and the fulfillment of our great prophecy." She paused, then continued, "Gareth and Cadence, you stand together today to join your hearts, souls, and our clan for eternity. Through the darkest of nights and the glorious of days, your union will ensure your strength. Your bond will forever protect you and your family. As our clan grows, your destiny will be fulfilled. May your lives be bountiful in love, laughter, and happiness."

Standing beside the couple were two pillars, each containing a single white candle. A tall gold candle sat on a higher pillar between them. Forcing back her tears, deep spiritual emotion poured through Carys. Watching her son, her forever, she nodded at the couple. "Each white candle represents your individual souls. By joining them, your souls become one.

Gazing into each other's eyes, Cadence and Gareth felt the love of their people and their ancestors encircle them. They each picked up one of the white candles and, holding their flames to the center candle, the fire lit. Shooting fire heavenward, they recited the words that would bind them forever. As the oath was taken, the glow from the firelight emanated out, encircling them.

Fated by fire, Forged in flames
Bound by blood, Lives forever changed
A passionate kiss to seal our fate
Starting a forever life anew
Unconditional love for thy mate
Fated by fire, Forged in flames
Bound by love
Eternally, two hearts now beat as one

The air around them sparked with energy and the magic hummed, building to a crescendo. The moment the vow they swore sealed their bond, Cadence and Gareth felt the backs of their necks begin to burn, joining their souls.

"Let me see, *un annwyl*," he whispered as he lifted her hair from her neck to stare at the beautiful mark. A Celtic Awen symbol with an exquisite set of dragon flames around it graced the back of her neck. The flames shot out from all directions, forging their mating. He knew that he had an identical symbol on his neck. It solidified their union, marking them as mates for the entire world to see.

Carys looked at them with love shining in her eyes. "The Awen is a symbol of the balance and harmony between the male and the female. The two outer lines symbolize the individual man and woman. The center line symbolizes the coming together of the two and the harmony that befits them. The dragon's flames around them are a symbol of our clan's immortality and holy tribute blessed to us by Merlin. The perfect combination that binds our family and our clan," her heart swelled with the happiness their future would bring.

Turning to face his mate Gareth took her hand in his, marveling in the softness of her skin. He held up a ring for her to see. A gorgeous ruby shone brightly in its center and was encircled by small emeralds. "This belonged to my grandmother and today I give it to you as a symbol of my love and eternal devotion. The ruby represents the fire that burns in our blood, and the emeralds represent the beauty of Wales." Slipping it onto her ring finger, he leaned down to gently kiss her hand. "From now until eternity, my life, my love, and my soul belong to you and only you. I promise to forever love you and protect you. I vow to never forsake you and to cherish you always."

Reaching into the hidden pocket in her dress, she drew her hand out. Opening her fingers, she picked up the ring that lay in the palm of her hand. "I found this in my grandmother's things. She left it for me to present to my future husband. It has been in our family for many generations. It was the ring her father gave her mother when they married. According to the note she left, it belonged to Merlin and was a symbol of our family's purity." She slid it onto his ring finger, feeling the spark of magic flare through her hand. Instead of scaring her, it filled her with a sense of warmth and ancestry. "I give this ring to you as a symbol of my love and devotion. I promise to spend the rest of my life treasuring and loving you. I give myself to you wholly for as long as I am alive. I will stand beside you through all life throws our way."

Closing the space between them, Gareth pulled Cadence into his arms. His lips found hers and he kissed her thoroughly. Devouring her mouth, his hands caressed her face.

Though Carys celebrated their mating, her mind was heavy with the danger surrounding them. Maelon and the *ddraig wen* wouldn't rest until their clan ruled, as they had long desired. She prayed that when the time came, their family would be strong enough to withstand the coming battle.

It was in the hands of Gareth and Cadence; they would take their clan into the next generations. They would rule with love, duty, and respect.

Stepping back from his mate, Gareth touched her chin. He expected the love and bond that would come with the mating, but the extreme devotion wasn't what he expected. His dragon would allow their mate to want for nothing.

Turning to face the crowd of family and clansmen, Cadence felt the love coming from the group. Taking Gareth's hand, they walked back towards the house. She could feel the tension in him. Could feel the distraction he was trying to hide from her. "Gareth, is everything okay?"

"Everything is wonderful, love. Today has been the perfect day," she reassured as he squeezed her hand.

"You don't lie worth a shit. Has anyone ever told you that?" she quipped, needing him to know she saw through him. "I know you're hiding something from me. And I want to know what it is!"

"It's really nothing, *un annwyl*. I'm just on edge. I don't want Maelon to have a chance to surprise us, but we aren't going to worry about him. We are going to spend the rest of the night celebrating our love and our mating with our friends and family. We aren't going to let him ruin our special day." Picking her up in his arms, he swung her around in circles until they were both dizzy.

Landing on the ground, Cadence broke out in giggles. Gareth rolled over on his side and planted a sweet kiss on the tip of her nose. "Are you ready to celebrate, *un annwyl*?"

"More than anything!" Getting to their feet, the couple headed to where to rest of their family and friends gathered to celebrate their mating.

The End

Thank you so much for reading Fated by Fire. I hope you enjoyed reading it as much I loved writing it. Please consider leaving a review. I appreciate and read all reviews.

A huge thank you to my cover designer, JC Clarke, and my editors, Laura Shaw and Kim Huther. They make me look great!

Thank you to my street team, TheZone! You're unwavering support and love touch me more than you know!

Want to keep up with me: Find me on Facebook and Twitter!

Facebook: https://www.facebook.com/KellyCozzoneAuthor
Twitter: https://twitter.com/KCozzone

Visit my website at http://kellycozzone.weebly.com/

Kelly's other books:

Romantic suspense thrillers:
Tropical Dreams
Tropical Nightmares

Coloring books:
Color Me Cursed

Cookbook:
Cooking with the Crazy Lady Authors

Coming Soon:
A Moment in Time
Tropical Paradise
Blind Attraction
Bound by Blood
A Whispered Christmas Wish

Made in the USA
San Bernardino, CA
27 January 2017